FeA

Retu
or an
Pleas
by pho

cu

fe

NANNY WANTED

Melbourne businesswoman, Elly George, has her life planned out. But then she employs Environmental Engineer and part-time nanny, Rusty Webster, to care for her eight-month-old god-child Molly. Living close together in her apartment, attraction and romance blossom. However, whilst Elly is an only child and career woman, Rusty comes from a large family and wants one of his own. Elly keeps her distance, believing that they are not suited. But is her career going to be enough for Elly?

*Books by Noelene Jenkinson
in the Linford Romance Library:*

NOELENE JENKINSON

NANNY WANTED

Complete and Unabridged

LINFORD
Leicester

First published in Great Britain in 2008

First Linford Edition
published 2008

British Library CIP Data

Jenkinson, Noelene
  Nanny wanted.—Large print ed.—
Linford romance library
  1. Businesswomen—Fiction 2. Male child
care workers—Fiction 3. Love stories
4. Large type books
  I. Title
823.9′2 [F]

ISBN 978–1–84782–452–3

Published by
F. A. Thorpe (Publishing)
Anstey, Leicestershire

Set by Words & Graphics Ltd.
Anstey, Leicestershire
Printed and bound in Great Britain by
T. J. International Ltd., Padstow, Cornwall

This book is printed on acid-free paper

1

Elly George jiggled her wailing eight-month-old goddaughter as she paced her Melbourne penthouse apartment.

She glanced through the wall of windows at the sweeping cityscape views. The thin landmark spire of the Arts Centre that pierced the blue morning sky like a mesh needle. Green and yellow trams clattering along St Kilda Road toward the city and across the Princes Bridge over the sluggish waters of the Yarra River.

The outside world seemed so detached and serene compared to the emotional upheaval in here. She turned her attention back to the baby, feeling helpless and incompetent. Compared to this, running her own company was a breeze. She'd left the hospital only hours before blissfully ignorant of the demands of minding a child.

'Molly, honey, you're a full-time job.' Elly contemplated the sweet red face and damp cheeks in despair.

At the sound of her godmother's voice, the squirming red-faced bundle stopped for a millisecond, her dark curly hair framing a tiny trusting face, her dusky eyelashes beaded with moisture.

Elly's office hours were hectic and loaded with the unexpected, but nothing she couldn't handle and nothing like this. She had tried bottles and a dummy, but nothing worked. Molly remained inconsolable.

Not surprising when she had been suddenly wrenched from her mother and everything familiar. As a result, Elly's day had deteriorated from chaotic to desperate. Finally, conceding she didn't have a single motherly gene in her body and unable to cope, she knew a decision had to be made. Fast.

That's when Plan B had entered her head. A nanny. Keeping the thought of Molly's welfare uppermost in her mind, Elly reminded herself this was an emergency and the phone call was a last resort. She took a deep calming breath, hitched the baby higher on her hip and pressed the rarely-dialled number of her mother's legal chambers.

'Emmanuelle.' Her mother's cultured voice eventually echoed in her ear. 'It's been too long, but we're all so busy, aren't we?'

Elly crushed the disappointment that her parents' lives had always revolved around work in preference to family.

'Mother, I'm minding Molly and — '

'Molly who?' she snapped.

'Molly Golding. Rachel's daughter.' She paused. 'My best friend from school,' she reminded her, exasperated.

'Of course,' her mother drawled with unconcealed contempt. 'The single mother on welfare. But why on earth are you minding her?'

'Rachel was in a car accident this morning.' She wondered if even that bad news would capture her mother's apathetic attention.

'Oh. How inconvenient for you.

Couldn't someone else have taken it?'

Her neglect in not asking after Rachel's condition, filled Elly with anger. 'Not it, Mother. She. Molly's a girl. And I offered to mind her. You know Rachel's parents live in Perth. She has no-one here. I couldn't let her down.'

'How long must you have her?' came her mother's pained voice as if Elly was asking her to mind the child herself.

'Ten days to a fortnight.'

'How can you possibly hope to succeed in your business burdened with a child?'

Strange, after almost a decade of hard work, she thought she'd already accomplished that. She flinched in the wake of the careless retort, but let it pass.

'You have no experience with children,' Louise stressed unkindly.

Elly inhaled another deep breath. 'I can learn. Meanwhile,' she continued crisply, 'A legislation of Canberra businessmen and ambassadors have arrived early and are waiting in my office as we speak. They weren't due for three hours so they've created an emergency. Against my better judgment, I'm hiring a nanny and I'd appreciate your recommendation of the best agency.'

'A sensible decision.' Her mother's voice crooned with silky pleasure. 'I know just the one.'

Elly heaved a grateful sigh, but felt a niggling sense of guilt over not being able to manage Molly herself.

There was a loaded pause. 'Angel Care,' she announced proudly, as though she'd just donated a substantial sum to charity.

'The best?'

'Would I ever recommend anything else?' Her mother sounded piqued. She relayed the telephone number and address then, without drawing breath, said, 'I must go, Emmanuelle. I have two calls on hold and clients waiting.'

As soon as she hung up, Elly swiftly dialled the nanny agency. She explained her urgent situation to a co-ordinator named Julie, praying she could help.

'For 24/7 care, Miss George, I'd recommend a nanny-housekeeper.' Elly's shoulders sagged in relief. Julie addressed her barrage of questions, then added with calm reassurance, 'Our staff are carefully screened and selected. We provide a top quality service.'

Elly was relieved to hear it for she would accept nothing less for Molly.

'Since it's an emergency,' Julie's professional voice continued, 'I'll send someone around to your apartment within the hour.'

Elly felt optimistic she could survive for another sixty minutes.

Carrying Molly and working single handed, one armful at a time, she transferred the child's mountain of paraphernalia from the tiled entry foyer where she had dumped it hours earlier after their arrival home from the hospital, into one of the two spare rooms.

Then she tried sitting Molly on her

own bedroom floor so she could change clothes ready for work, but the wailing recommenced so Elly scooped her up again. If comfort and cuddles were the only solution, then that's how it would be.

She shook her head and embraced a whole ton of respect for mothers everywhere. Her heartstrings tugged at Molly's distress. Instant motherhood was a steep learning curve.

Sixty-five minutes later, Elly anxiously marched around the apartment still nursing Molly. 'She's coming.' Surely she couldn't be far away?

Even as she spoke, the classical melody of her doorbell chimed. Elly strode across her apartment to the hall and checked the peephole.

She groaned at the sight of a tall raven-haired man carrying an official-looking briefcase. A door-to-door salesman at this hour? How had he passed security? And why did companies always send such Greek gods to sell their products? A

7

marketing strategy perhaps?

Firmly clutching Molly, she jerked open the door with her free hand, deciding firstly to get rid of this stranger fast and secondly to complain to the management.

'Whatever you're selling, I'm not interested.' Elly tried slamming the door in the caller's rather handsome suntanned face, but he jammed his foot in the narrowing gap.

'Mrs George?'

The voice was deep and educated and calm. And knew her? His confidence threw Elly off balance until a tweak of suspicion eased into her mind. He couldn't be! But for good measure she checked.

'And you are?'

'Rusty Webster. I'm from Angel Care.'

Elly curbed her surprise and almost dropped Molly. A male nanny? Well, this was the 21st century, but weren't they usually younger? This guy had to be on the scary side of thirty.

He extended a large hand. Still stunned by his appearance when she'd been expecting a female, Elly accepted it, vaguely aware of its size and warmth covering hers.

'And this will be Molly?' He gazed warmly across at her and slid a finger into the child's tiny hand. Molly gripped it tight. Webster's lopsided smile was wide and genuine, revealing perfect teeth.

'Correct,' Elly said with cool reserve.

He was utterly unruffled as her critical gaze of inspection skimmed him up and down. His longish black wavy hair almost touched his shoulders, was neatly styled but needed a decent cut, and dark twinkling eyes measured her in return.

'Well, Mr Webster,' she said ungraciously, 'You'd better come in.'

Rusty noticed with pleasure that his potential employer equalled his height and looked directly into his eyes. Rather chilly blue eyes. He bet they could sparkle with fun if she wanted.

Even carrying a child, she took long easy strides and moved with a swift lithe grace. A classy woman, but then his occasional temporary employers usually were.

He closed the door and followed her into a huge luxurious sunken sitting-room. Every piece of furniture was precisely placed. No magazines cluttered the glass coffee table and no toys littered the floor. It sure looked like no-one really lived here.

The carpet was so soft his shoes sank and it cushioned his tread. It reminded him of walking in loose sand. Ideal for a crawling infant. Rusty glanced across at Molly in her mother's arms.

The apartment's most sensational feature was a stunning wall of windows with uninterrupted city and horizon views.

He gave a soft appreciative whistle. 'Lovely place you have here.'

Mrs George stepped down into the formally arranged conversation area and spun around to face him, struggling with her writhing child. The light caught her hair, warming it with gold as it swung about her shoulders.

'Thank you.' She seemed surprised by his compliment and her clear blue eyes shone with a touch of pride. 'Please, sit down.'

Rusty frowned. Somehow, this lady didn't fit the usual mould. He nodded and perched opposite on the edge of a cream leather sofa, unlatched his briefcase and withdrew his references. 'These should tell you everything you need to know about my experience and qualifications.'

As the woman took his file, he noticed no wedding rings on her long slender fingers. Maybe she was a single mother. Even in jeans and a T-shirt, wearing no make-up and with red-painted toenails on her enticingly bare feet, the woman was a stunner. Well bred and educated. If he ever found a female like this one, he'd make it official pretty quick, whip a ring on her finger and do everything in his power to show her he cared and keep her for life. If she was unattached, she was available. Rusty's imagination was teased by the possibility.

In vain, the woman tried opening his folder with Molly in her arms. 'If you'll bear with me while I read through all your paperwork, I'll get down to questions and specifics shortly.' She flashed a stiff polite smile.

He shrugged and lounged back against the deep sofa. 'No rush. Take all the time you need.'

He might as well enjoy the comfort while he was here. Ms George doubted his ability for the job, but she'd change her mind after reading his resume. He let his gaze roam the room. Given the chance, he'd appreciate living here for a few weeks before he roughed it in the Outback.

As Molly struggled in the woman's lap, she kicked the folder and papers whooshed in a cloud of white sheets across the floor.

'Oh, no . . . ' She sighed with exasperation.

Rusty leapt to his feet, picked up each scattered page and sorted them into order again. Good thing they were numbered. He replaced the folder on the glass table before her.

'No harm done,' he smiled easily. 'If you agree, Ms George, I'd be happy to hold Molly for you while you read.'

Relief and gratitude spread across her face. Slowly, she raised the child from her lap and handed Molly across to him. 'Thank you. That would be a big help.'

'My pleasure.' Rusty reached out and accepted the child. 'Hi, Angel,' he greeted her gently.

The child's bottom lip quivered but no tears fell as she warily stared at her new minder. She seemed unusually upset and he wondered what had triggered the problem.

He glanced up and caught Ms George gaping at him until she whipped away her gaze and reached for his folder. No doubt sizing him up for the job. About two weeks, Julie thought. If he was acceptable. Which fitted in nicely before his Northern Territory job.

As Rusty cuddled Molly against him and massaged her back, the woman cleared her throat. 'Mr Webster.' She distractedly leafed through his reference papers, hesitating, keeping her gaze downcast. 'Molly's not my daughter. She's my godchild. My best friend, Rachel's daughter.' Finally, she looked up at him. 'It's Miss not Mrs, and it's quite acceptable if you call me Elly.'

He raised his eyebrows in interest. He knew it. All the pieces of the puzzle fit together. He hadn't read her wrong after all. 'Of course. And you can call me Rusty.'

Molly had quietened so he carefully turned and cradled her in his arms. Before long, a small thumb found its way into her mouth, her eyelids grew heavy and fluttered closed.

'The little traitor,' Elly scoffed in disbelief. 'You seem to have a rapport with children,' she observed wistfully.

He thought about it. 'Perhaps.'

'Tell me, Rusty, whyever did you become a nanny?'

He shrugged. 'I've always loved kids. I grew up the oldest in a big family and amused my younger siblings. Now, I have nine nieces and nephews, and I help out my sister, Julie, at the agency when she needs it. She started Angel Care five years ago and I offered my support.'

Elly's gaze sharpened and her head tilted to one side, assessing. 'Julie at the agency is your sister?'

He nodded. 'Yes, that's right.'

Her fingers drummed a beat on his reference papers. 'That could be considered favouritism.'

'It could,' he drawled. 'Except I have years of experience and have completed all the training to gain official qualification.' His cool gaze challenged hers and his jaw clenched. 'I don't take this job lightly.'

Elly glared back at him without

remorse. 'I should hope not.'

'Nannies must meet strict criteria. A mandatory minimum number of years childcare experience. I've gained a paediatric first aid certificate and undergone a full reference investigation.' He nodded toward the folder of papers spread across her lap. 'As you can see from the letters of verification in my resume.'

'I noticed,' she grudgingly admitted.

'We also undergo a national police and criminal clearance, and driving history check,' he added, toning down the defensive bite in his voice.

'Your agency appears extremely thorough.' She paused. 'As I would expect.'

She still sounded prickly and an aggressive glint sparkled in her eyes. He'd like to have this tenacious woman on his side in a predicament.

'How long do you plan on staying in this kind of work?'

Whatever her reason for posing the question, his answer was easy. 'I'll continue as long as Julie needs me.'

'I wouldn't have thought being a nanny was a career choice for a man.'

At the risk of losing the job, Rusty bristled. 'It's a worthy and skilled vocation, whether a man or a woman does it. Don't you think it's important?'

'Certainly.'

'And you have to admit it's not easy or you'd be doing the job yourself and not considering hiring me.'

Shocked by his honesty, she gaped, lost for words. He couldn't resist adding, 'I'm also a qualified Environmental Engineer.'

Her slim eyebrows flickered upwards and he knew she was impressed. 'Indeed.' She paused, scrambling for words. 'Well, Mr Webster.' Her soft voice remained firm. 'Since your credentials appear to be in order, I have decided to employ you.'

Rusty wanted to punch the air and shout, 'Yes!' but because Molly slept in his arms, he nodded and said gratefully, 'Thank you, Elly.'

'Don't make me regret it.'

2

Elly glanced across at Rusty Webster and understood his defence of being a nanny. She hadn't meant to degrade his second job choice. She'd merely needed to establish his sincerity in the work.

With her own succession of nannies throughout childhood, she appreciated they served a purpose, but they could never replace a parent's love. It would have been so much easier if she could have taken Molly to work, and comforting, knowing she was nearby. Especially when the child wasn't her own and she felt doubly responsible.

Rusty's environmental career suited him, she decided. He was the rugged outdoor type. All the more wonder then because the vision opposite presented a touching sight; a big man gently and capably holding a baby. The soft trusting bundle sleeping contentedly in his arms.

Elly collected her thoughts and concluded the interview. 'I'm usually absent from around seven each morning but, while Molly's here, I can stretch it to seven-thirty or eight.'

'No problem. I understand you need me to live in.'

'In the evenings.' She hesitated. 'I finish when I'm done. At the moment in my business, it's a particularly busy time. I'm investigating national expansion.'

'And yet you took on even more responsibility with Molly.' His gaze narrowed. 'Rash move.'

'I'm used to making snap decisions in business,' she countered. 'It was the only one to make.'

He paused. 'Can I ask where Molly's mother is?'

Elly set Rusty's folder on the table and sighed. 'It's an unfortunate story.'

Reliving the incident, she recounted the morning crisis. The early phone call and alarm at hearing of a nasty car accident in peak hour traffic. The dash to the hospital not knowing what to expect when she arrived.

'Rachel was covered with blood.' She rubbed her arms, shivering in recollection. 'Fortunately it looked worse than it actually was. The doctors diagnosed broken bones and minor internal injuries. Molly miraculously escaped unscathed. Rachel was fretting about her while she was in hospital. Rachel's a single mum and we've been best friends since school,' Elly explained, 'so it seemed natural for me to mind her baby for the duration.'

'A challenging start to the day,' Rusty agreed. 'Will your friend be OK?'

The beginnings of hesitant respect stirred in Elly. His interest showed compassion, a sentiment her own mother had lacked.

She nodded. 'Thankfully, yes.'

Elly was grateful for a nanny's help. Besides covering her work commitments, she craved the support. She had always felt intimidated by children, especially babies, although she would never admit it.

It proved a daunting thought to be sharing her home with a man and child, but this was for Molly's benefit, and she would adjust.

Elly unwound her long limbs from the sofa. 'I'd best show you around the apartment.'

'Sure.' His sudden smile filled the room with a congenial warmth. Its effect reinforced her decision to hire him and banished her previous concerns.

She checked her wristwatch. 'Then I must dash. I have less than an hour to make that meeting. I have two spare bedrooms; one can be used as a nursery, the other will be yours.'

Rusty transferred Molly to rest snugly against his shoulder. Her gaze lingered over the sight and a roll of warmth ran through her. They looked so cute together.

'I hope I brought everything Molly

needs from Rachel's flat,' she said briskly over her shoulder as she led the way across the sitting room toward the bedroom wing.

She opened a door and moved aside to let Rusty enter with Molly. He stepped around the collapsed cot on the floor. Bags of disposable nappies and baby clothes were strewn all over the double bed, and a folded stroller leant against a wall.

'I can't believe such a small person needs all this.' Elly smiled weakly, stretching a hand around the room.

Rusty cast his gaze about. 'Looks to be all here. I'll settle Molly and organise everything while you get ready for work.'

He sounded so competent and Molly was so content, Elly's spirits lifted. What more could she ask? 'Are you sure?'

'Absolutely.'

She hadn't realised he was standing so close, caught her breath and stepped back. Molly was still nestled sleepily against him. A cosy place to be, she imagined, supported by two big strong hands and arms.

Suddenly realising she was staring and irritated by her lapse in concentration, she mumbled excuses and escaped, dashing down the hall to her bedroom suite. Before she showered, she called her personal assistant, Dallas, to tell her she was finally on her way.

Twenty minutes later, the transformation from sloppy home clothes to business persona was complete. Elly tossed her cosmetics, laptop and mobile into her briefcase, smoothed her tights and slid her feet into black high heeled pumps.

She strode back down the hall and peeped around the nursery door, gaping at its swift conversion. Molly slept in the portable cot and all the remaining paraphernalia was neatly stowed away.

In the face of such daunting domestic efficiency, she ran a hand over her hair, tugged at the tailored jacket of her classic designer suit and cleared her throat.

'Rusty?'

She winced at the familiarity of using his first name. He seemed to have sensed her presence because he looked up even as she spoke. His dark compelling eyes held hers, giving the impression of seeing her for the first time. His warm brown eyes travelled over her a number of times before settling on her lips which she had given a lavish coat of cranberry gloss to match her outfit.

She found his stare unsettling and glanced toward Molly.

He followed her gaze and cast a fond look down at his tiny charge. 'She's exhausted. She'll sleep for hours.'

Elly lowered her voice. 'Would you like the rest of that apartment tour now?'

He nodded and stepped forward, closer, invading her personal space again. 'Good idea. I just need to find the laundry and kitchen for Molly's clothes and meals.'

'Your room's at the end of the hall.' She gestured as he followed. 'And this is the bathroom.'

She opened the door and entered. The walls were light blue, the tiling white and the fittings gold. A massive hand painted coral reef mural covered the far wall, lifting the elegant room to spectacular. 'You'll find fresh towels and supplies in the hall cupboard.'

'Nice,' he murmured and a restrained grin twitched the corners of his mouth.

He brushed against her as they stood in the centre of the floor and Elly flinched. Unnerved by the contact, her heels clattered on the tiled floor with the movement, making her appear gauche.

'Dangerous things.' He looked down at her shoes and chuckled, then glanced back again.

Elly found herself breathless. 'Let's continue, shall we?'

In the kitchen, Rusty's eyes followed

her as she explained the layout and appliances.

When she was done, he leant against the bench top, arms and legs easily crossed. Beneath the down lights, she noticed auburn lights spark fiery highlights through his long dark hair.

'Are you all right?' he asked suddenly, his deep voice softer. 'I mean after the accident, seeing Rachel injured and bringing Molly home. I imagine it was quite unsettling for you.'

She blinked back surprise at his concern. It had indeed. Since her neglect in childhood, Elly had learnt to stifle her emotions, and cope alone.

Quite frankly, she longed to kick off her shoes, lounge on the sofa with a coffee and a thick read, forgetting work for a change. But she never found time for such luxuries any more.

'I'm fine.' Elly shut down any hint of sentiment or regret, unzipped the side pouch on her briefcase and withdrew a business card. 'You can reach me on any of these numbers any time. My office, my mobile and my secretary.'

Rusty accepted it, twirling it deftly in his fingers. 'I can have a simple meal ready when you get home,' he suggested.

The comment emerged from nowhere and caught her off guard. 'You can?' With nowhere else to look or turn, Elly found herself drawn once again into the sparkling depths of those dark eyes.

He shrugged easily. 'It looks like you're in for a long day and I imagine you'll be beat by the end of it. I'm happy to help out. Any duties apart from caring for Molly are up for negotiation with my employer.'

Tempting and generous. 'It's not necessary. I usually don't eat much.'

His gaze flickered over her again. 'I can see that. All the same, I'll prepare something light. Just in case,' he murmured.

Standing in the kitchen feeling lost and vulnerable in her own home, Elly focused on formality to halt being sucked in by the gentle reassurance in his deep voice. 'Only if you have time. Molly comes first.'

'Of course.' His quick frown mocked her.

His teasing annoyed her and she scowled. 'I'll see you tonight.'

'We'll be here.'

As she turned and walked out of the apartment, Elly found his quiet statement strangely comforting.

In the basement car park, Elly slid into the leather seat of her BMW coupé and phoned her office.

'Dallas? I'm in my car. Depending on traffic, I should be about fifteen minutes. I assume they're waiting?'

'Yes. Lapping up the view, your coffee and the gourmet lunch I ordered in,' came her strong voice. 'Has to beat airline food.'

Retrenched from her previous job, Dallas had re-trained in the Academy, one of the first graduates five years ago. Elly had snapped her up and they had become a complementary team ever since.

'You're an angel. Remind me to give you a raise.'

'I do. Regularly.' She chuckled before hanging up.

Twenty minutes later, Elly breezed into her office.

'Molly OK?' Dallas asked, rising from her desk and striding after her boss into the adjoining office.

Elly nodded.

'Nanny finally arrive?'

Elly nodded again.

'Wouldn't have been a problem if we had a crèche,' Dallas teased.

Elly groaned as she removed papers from her briefcase. 'Don't start that campaign again. Now is not the time. Every spare cent of capital is committed to development.' She nodded toward the meeting room down the hall. 'Everything ready in there?'

Dallas nodded. Elly noticed her assistant's sporty curls shone with an auburn rinse to camouflage the creeping grey of middle age which the older woman struggled to conceal. A smart black trouser suit slimmed down her mature figure.

'New outfit?' Elly raised her eyebrows in appreciation.

'I found it on sale in Myers.' Dallas slowly turned around to give her boss a comprehensive view. 'What do you think?'

'Snappy. And that silk scarf is a bright touch. Am I paying you enough to afford that?'

Dallas grimaced. 'No, but it was such a bargain, I couldn't leave it in the store.'

Elly grabbed her papers and took a deep breath. 'OK. Let's go charm those male suits.'

Throughout the meeting, and during her presentation and question time afterwards, Elly's thoughts wandered back to her apartment. How was Rusty coping? Was Molly still asleep?

Distracted, she stumbled over a word here, a fact there, but covered it all with a smile and the smooth professionalism that was not only her own personal hallmark, but also a distinctive attribute of every person that graduated from her Gold Staff Academy.

Later, as she waded through e-mails, phone calls and the morning post, Dallas sailed into her office with the usual wholemeal gourmet salad sandwich and daily indulgent mocha latte ordered in from her favourite nearby café.

Elly looked up, her hands pausing over the computer keyboard. 'Thanks.'

Dallas planted her hands on her hips and assumed motherly concern. 'You really should try the outdoors sometimes for a break. You know, sunshine and fresh air?' she chided.

Elly glanced at the superb view across the Yarra River and hungrily scooped her lunch out of it's trendy monogrammed cardboard box. 'I can see it from here. My home gym's just fine.'

'Your business is established and humming now,' her assistant muttered. 'You should slow down and delegate.'

Elly was well aware that, now Dallas' four sons were grown, she itched for more responsibility and promotion.

'Maybe,' she gave a tolerant smile, shrugging aside her concerns. 'But I enjoy it so much.'

'You have enough to manage already,' Dallas argued, 'If you expand, you'll never cope alone. Unless you give up eating and sleeping.' She gathered up the latest batch of signed correspondence to mail.

'Point taken. But stop worrying about me.'

Dallas shrugged. 'I'm a mother. We're born to worry. You should make time for other things in your life.'

'Like family?' Elly's mouth curled into an ironic twist. 'You have a devoted husband and family, plus parents that care.'

'I'm sure your folks care,' she said carefully. 'They just don't show it.'

'You think so?' Elly's eyebrows crinkled with doubt.

'You have Rachel,' Dallas reminded

her. 'Speaking of your friend, I hope they nail that guy who ran the red light and put her in hospital. She is going to be OK?' Dallas queried in a stern voice.

Elly finished munching her first mouthful of lunch and nodded. 'Fortunately. Might take a while though.' She sipped her mocha latte, closed her eyes for a moment and enjoyed the rich flavour as it slid down her throat. 'The hospital says she could be hospitalised for up to two weeks.'

'You're lucky you can afford a nanny to help out.'

Elly flashed her assistant a dark look. 'Don't even go there.'

She was sympathetic to the idea of an office crèche. With mainly female staff and trainees, Elly appreciated there might be a need but didn't have time right now to study its feasibility.

'I know.' Dallas raised a hand in mock surrender and grinned. 'Just keeping the idea in your mind. So, what's she like?'

'Who?' Elly deliberately played for time.

'The nanny.'

Elly pretended to be searching through the mountain of papers on her desk to keep her eyes downcast. 'Actually . . . it's a man.'

Dallas' eyes lit up and she beamed. 'No way.'

Elly took advantage of her gaping reaction and rare speechless moment. 'So, if you take any phone calls from a Mr Rusty Webster, put him through immediately, OK? No matter where I am, who I'm with or what I'm doing.'

'Sure.' Dallas regarded her boss closely and probed further. 'How old is this nanny anyway?'

Elly wasn't in the mood for even good-natured teasing about her non-existent social life and didn't elaborate on the fact that her nanny was way beyond his teens and good-looking to boot. So she opted for evasion.

'Old enough, and experienced.' She pointed to the thick open diary Dallas clutched to her chest. 'Tell me about the rest of today.'

Skilfully diverted, Dallas launched into a résumé of afternoon appointments and teaching classes.

Before her first deportment and etiquette class, Elly reduced her pile of correspondence. Too often, her concentration lapsed and she stared idly out of her window, chewed on her pen and doodled on her notepad. Finally relenting, she picked up the phone.

'George apartment.'

'Rusty, it's Elly. How's it going?'

'Afternoon. Nice to hear from you.'

It sounded so good to hear his deep warm voice again. Of course. It was reassuring to know someone so reliable was caring for Molly.

'Molly slept well and she's much brighter. She's just eaten lunch and now we're playing. She'll probably go down for another nap soon, but we'll play it by ear.'

'I'm relieved she's happier and more settled.' Elly scowled. 'I was so worried before you arrived.'

'I know. That's natural.'

His tactful assurance lifted her mood. 'I'll see you tonight.'

After hanging up, Elly returned to work with renewed concentration and actually looked forward to returning home. Normally, there was no enticement or rush.

She remembered that Rusty had promised to prepare dinner and tried to recall if there was enough food in the refrigerator or pantry to make a decent meal. She groaned. There might be a Lean Cuisine dinner in the freezer.

Later, Elly phoned the Alfred Hospital to be told Rachel was improving and could receive visitors tomorrow.

Because she'd had a late start that morning, it was almost eight and dark before she left the office and drove home. As she approached the six storey glass-fronted apartment building, Elly glowed with pride and satisfaction. Her luxurious home was a measure of her personal success.

Although mentally beat, Elly's weariness was forgotten as she rode the elevator upstairs. It seemed forever since she'd left this morning.

She unlocked the front door and dumped her briefcase and holdall bag on the floor. In the hall, she flipped off her shoes, leaning against the wall while she massaged her aching feet. She didn't hear or see anything as she padded barefoot across the living room, but light flooded from the kitchen and heavenly smells drifted into her senses. Elly spread neatening fingers through her hair and straightened her suit before stepping into the kitchen.

Rusty turned at her approach. 'Evening, Ms George,' he said with mock formality, addressing her more like a friend than an employee.

The down lights gleamed on his dark hair, making it appear shades lighter. He still wore the same clothes but he looked fresh and vital.

A quick glance around the room

revealed a big dish of something cooking in the oven, a glass bowl of salad prepared on the bench, and the dining table set with candles.

Elly was amused at her designer chef's kitchen actually being used for once and determined to enjoy it while it lasted. She backed up against the counter and folded her arms, disregarding the day's rushed start and long hours.

'Hi,' was all she could say, feeling like a stranger.

'So, how was Monday?' he asked.

'Chaotic as usual.' She managed a tentative smile.

'I noticed a bottle of white in the refrigerator. Would you like me to pour a glass?'

She nodded. 'Thanks. Where's Molly?'

'Asleep already. She had a brief nap after you telephoned.' His mouth tugged into a reflective smile as he poured the wine. 'But she could hardly keep her eyes open beyond seven. I didn't want to keep her up.'

Elly endured a twinge of disappointment. 'No, of course not. Her needs come first.'

He handed her the drink. 'I wasn't sure how late you'd be.'

'Thanks.'

Elly savoured the liquid and let it sharpen her taste buds. 'What's on the menu?' she asked, bending to peek in the oven.

'Beef burgundy and Mediterranean salad.' He grinned. 'I ordered some groceries. Receipts are in your office.'

'Fine.' She nodded. 'Sounds and smells delicious.'

She contemplated him, a hand towel tucked into the waistband of his trousers and dangling at his side, until he caught her staring and she quickly looked away.

'I managed some time on the laptop while Molly slept this afternoon. I'm in the middle of working up recommendations on a Northern Territory assignment.'

A man of many talents who combined both fields of endeavour with ease. But while he was in her employ, she'd rather he focused on childcare. 'As long as it doesn't interfere with this job. Molly comes first.'

'Always.' He glowered at her reproach then wiped his hands on the towel hitched to his belt. 'Dinner's ready. Do you want to take ten minutes to unwind or eat now?'

'I'll look in on Molly first.'

He shrugged. 'You're the boss.'

3

When Elly set down her glass and ambled from the kitchen, she cringed to discover Rusty trailing behind. She had hoped to see her godchild alone. For one single disturbing reason. To her growing alarm, whenever she was around him, she was so overcome by his deep mellow voice and stunning smile, her chest tightened and she forgot to breathe. The guy couldn't help it, she supposed, if he radiated a larrikin charm. He wasn't her type, but he held a dangerous kind of forbidden fascination.

She reminded herself he was here temporarily to do a job and she would never see him again.

As she leaned over Molly's cot, Rusty hovered nearby. Her senses shot to attention like radar sending out pulse waves, detecting his presence.

She took deep calming breaths and focused on Molly. Pink cheeked and sucking a thumb, she slept soundly, her dark hair like Rachel's, curled sweetly about her serene little face. Looking helpless and dependent, smelling sweet and clean, Elly could see that babies weren't so bad after all. They grew on you.

'She looks utterly content.' She lowered her voice. 'Thank you for taking care of her for me.'

'It's my job,' he muttered.

A twinge of reality darted through her and she half-turned to him. 'Yes, it is, but I wish I could have cared for her myself.'

'That's understandable.' His reassurance was quietly calming.

'I called the hospital this evening and Rachel's allowed visitors tomorrow.'

He nodded. 'Sounds encouraging. You must be relieved.'

'Yes.' She hesitated, touched by his concern. 'I'll go and change for dinner.'

Elly undressed and hung up her suit,

then zipped into a pair of casual black trousers and buttoned up a soft honey-coloured knit that hugged her body, slipping her feet into soft leather mules.

When she reappeared in the kitchen, Rusty was dishing up the casserole, the crisp salad already piled into a side dish.

Watching him as he worked, Elly figured there had to be a woman in his life. No domestic saint like this remained unattached.

'Have you already eaten?' She strolled after him into the dining-room, noticing only one place set at the table.

'No.'

'Please, you've made ample. Won't you join me?' She hesitated. 'Or is that not usually done.'

'Depends on the family and if I'm asked.' He sank his hands into his pockets.

'Well, since I usually eat alone, consider yourself invited. I'd be pleased to share your company.'

'Thanks.' He grinned. 'I didn't want to presume. I'll be right back.' He strode into the kitchen and returned with his own plate of food, a set of cutlery and another place mat.

After her first mouthful, Elly raised her glass in recognition of his efforts. 'This is delicious.' Then blurted out, 'Do you have a family?'

At her innocent query, his body stiffened and his natural easy manner disappeared. 'No.'

Elly was shocked to hear it and, because of his reaction, wished she hadn't asked.

After a long pause, he added, 'But I have four sisters and they're all married with kids.'

'Wow.' Hit with a healthy dose of envy, Elly marvelled how much more fun it would have been growing up with siblings. 'How did you become a nanny?'

'After my divorce two years ago, I became a bit of a hermit so my sister

Julie took me up as a cause.'

The word divorce hit Elly like a blast of cold air. Then he spoke of being dragged into babysitting, kindergarten, playground and car pools. He made it sound an imposition, but deep affection lurked behind his words.

'Next thing I knew,' Rusty continued, 'I'd completed nanny and childcare courses, and my name was on Julie's agency register as an emergency.'

Elly became fascinated by him as they ate. The play of light on his hair, the way his mouth moved and the way his big tanned hands deftly handled his food. Married and divorced by thirty. Not unusual in these times of less stable relationships.

'Did it work?'

'Minding children was wonderful therapy.' After a while, Rusty said quietly, 'I plan to try again.' His big brown eyes reflected a steely glint of determination, but the tone of his voice was still defined by sadness.

Her compassion sharpened. 'Remarry?

You're a brave man.'

'Next time, I'll make sure I pick the right woman.'

His statement carried a bitter edge. His warm eyes had cooled and Elly noticed he no longer smiled. He seemed so decided about the future and his fierce resolve hit her with a jolt of reality. Her own plans couldn't be more different.

'What's in your crystal ball of life?' Rusty asked suddenly.

'My business career,' Elly stated without hesitation, placing her cutlery neatly together on her empty plate.

'Nothing more?'

Elly noted the insinuation and bristled. 'Isn't that enough?'

He hedged. 'For some women maybe.'

'You don't think ambition's acceptable for a woman?'

'I didn't say that.'

A twinge of disquiet settled in her chest and she couldn't understand why. 'Considering you've crossed over the boundaries yourself into a traditional female domain, your views seem rather narrow. We're all individuals and we each have personal goals and needs. I've worked hard to build a successful business. It's my life.'

'I thought your biological clock might be ticking over,' he quipped.

'Give me a break,' she snapped. 'I'm not thirty. I have plenty of time.'

He grinned. 'I understand it can hit a woman when she least expects it.'

'Don't look at me like that. I have a company to run and expansion on the horizon.'

A stack of paperwork and files waited, so she rose from the table and took her dishes into the kitchen.

Rusty appeared behind her. 'I noticed some chocolate fudge ice-cream in the freezer. Want some?'

'I don't eat dessert. I keep it for Rachel. But, please,' she swept her arm toward the refrigerator. 'If you want some, help yourself.'

'I believe I will,' he drawled, throwing

her a loaded glance, and Elly suspected he wasn't just referring to the ice-cream. 'I'll do the dishes.'

Besides not being any good with babies, Elly also avoided kitchens. 'Great. Thanks for dinner. It was very . . . tasty. When did you learn to cook?'

Rusty chuckled softly as he rinsed plates and cutlery. 'My mother encouraged us as soon as we could to peel potatoes and see over the kitchen bench. In a family of seven, everyone helped.'

His homely upbringing sounded cosy and fun. Not for the first time, Elly experienced a faint twist on envy. 'Well, I have work to do.'

'Me too.' She halted mid-step. 'Oh?'

'Still have my report to finish,' he said over the clatter of dishes and running water.

'Do you need a place to work?'

'No. I'll work on the living-room sofa, same as today.'

Elly cringed and caught herself before she spilled out an objection to his messing up the apartment. Instead, she theoretically bit her tongue and smiled.

As she settled down to work in her office, she remembered the sweeping critical look Rusty had given her apartment this morning when he first arrived and it wasn't envy. Well, she liked neat. Her concentration wandered as she tried to work. She usually enjoyed the peace and city lights blinking back at her but tonight felt restless. An hour and a half later, it was with an odd sense of relief she welcomed an interruption. There was a firm rap at her door and Rusty entered.

'I brewed coffee. Want some?'

Elly stretched, pushed back her swivel chair and rose to her feet. 'Desperately.'

She caught Rusty watching her, but ignored it because it made her feel too feminine and not like his employer.

He pulled his gaze away and nodded to the blaze of city lights below. 'It's an even better view at night.'

'Hmm, fabulous.'

He took a step toward the door then hesitated. 'You don't ever crave a garden and lawn?'

She pushed back her hair and sighed. 'I wouldn't have time to weed and mow.'

His eyes shone over her. 'Maybe your man would.'

Her man. An ideal unlikely to materialise any time soon. 'Maybe.' Her voice emerged soft and husky.

Without another word, Rusty left, leaving Elly to briefly contemplate the fantasy before muttering, 'Get real,' and wandering into the living-room to join him.

A tray laid out with coffee mugs, milk and sugar was already set down on the glass table.

Rusty sprawled out full length on one of the sofas and watched her approach. Elly found his scrutiny unnerving. She'd never met a person who so thoroughly infiltrated her senses.

She bristled with irritation at the

sight of his belongings untidily strewn across her piece of designer furniture. Alongside his laptop computer, mobile phone and papers scattered about, huge unrolled plans of some kind were casually anchored at each end by her two weighted silver candlesticks, usually displayed on top of the glass table with a little more finesse.

Elly's annoyance dissolved as she inhaled the pungent aroma of fresh coffee and experienced the business end of his stunning smile.

She curled her feet beneath her and settled on the opposite sofa. 'Did you finish your report?'

Rusty regarded her over the top of his mug, intense dark eyes, watching. 'Should wrap it up tomorrow while Molly's asleep.'

'What exactly does your environmental work involve?' She wrapped her hands around the mug and blew on the hot drink to cool it.

'An initial approach from a potential employer.'

'Such as?'

He shrugged. 'The energy industry or a mining company. I work on contract as a consultant for each project. This time, he nodded toward his paperwork, 'It's a cattle station in the Territory.'

His work sounded important and worthwhile. 'Then what?'

'I travel out to the location for an inspection and take surveys of the surrounding geographical features. Then I assess the effect of the proposed activity on the environment, and any sensitive flora and fauna.' He shrugged. 'If there's a potential problem, I develop methods of minimising impact and provide a comprehensive report.'

'So you don't just tell them what they want to hear.'

'I've never been a 'yes' man. That would defeat the purpose of employing me in the first place.' He changed the subject. 'By the way, I took the liberty of parking my vehicle down in the basement.'

'Sure. Give me the registration and I'll phone security.'

'Dark green RV.' He grinned. 'And it needs a wash.'

He retrieved a pen from among his papers, flipped open a notebook and scrawled. He tore off the page and handed it across the table. As she reached over to accept it, their fingers brushed. At the warm touch, Elly's body sparked in reaction. She snatched away her hand, folded the paper and pushed it into her trouser pocket.

She cleared her throat and continued as though nothing had happened. 'I suppose you get out into the country a lot with your work?'

'Sure do. Beats city traffic jams.'

'You said this morning you live in the Yarra Valley, didn't you?' Elly shamelessly fished, wanting to know more about him.

'That's right.' His lips tilted into an amused grin.

Elly cringed. Did he suspect her curiosity was personal? 'Do your sisters live in Melbourne?'

He nodded. 'Two live in the eastern suburbs and the other two live further south on the Mornington Peninsula.'

'And your folks?'

'Not far from me. In Healesville. Every second Sunday the tribe descends on them for lunch. It's a circus.' He chuckled, 'But it makes sure we all keep in touch.'

Elly compared the Websters' open house attitude with her own parents' formality. She was rarely invited home and children scampering about threatening their precious antiques would be forbidden.

'How many are there in your family when you get together?' Elly asked, imagining multitudes.

Rusty's eyes lit up. 'There's twenty of us and I'm an uncle to nine of the little critters.' Rusty's face shone with quiet pride. 'My youngest sister is expecting her second child soon.'

'Quite an achievement, and a crowd.' Elly marvelled at the thought.

'Are you an auntie?'

She smiled weakly and tried not to feel inadequate. 'No. I'm an only child.'

Elly wished she could brag about siblings. Rusty made his family sound wonderful. She was unprepared for the sympathetic look he cast in her direction. 'Really? You must have been lonely.'

Elly shook her head and skirted the truth. 'I had friends at school.' She had compensated by concentrating on her studies.

'Rachel?'

Elly nodded.

'So, a big responsibility rests on your shoulders to produce grandchildren for them?'

'I'm not planning any, but my parents won't be disappointed. To them, success is more important than family.' Elly failed to keep a tinge of regret from her voice.

He regarded her solemnly. 'Is that why you work so hard? Expectations?'

His question made her think. Had

she subconsciously strived to please? Elly shrugged amid troubled thoughts. 'Perhaps.'

'What do they do?'

'My father's a surgeon and my mother's a barrister. They live and practice in Toorak.'

Rusty's eyebrows raised in recognition of the affluent suburb then he stretched his long limbs, flexed his muscles and set his empty coffee mug on the table. Sitting forward in his seat, he rested his elbows on his knees and clasped his hands. 'So, you're not planning to add to the world's population?' A hint of amazement entered his voice.

Niggled by his challenge, Elly retorted, 'No.'

'What happens if you meet a guy and fall in love and he wants a family?'

No man yet had ever made her heart race, although Webster had snagged her attention more than most, but he wasn't a likely candidate.

'I wouldn't let a relationship develop

that far. Besides, I'm perfectly content with my life.'

'For now. What about the future?'

'I prefer to live in the present,' she flashed back.

'There's a lot to be said for loving someone and expressing that love with a family.'

'It didn't work in your marriage.'

The instant the words left her mouth, Elly wished them back. Rusty winced before he clenched his jaw and his dark eyes shadowed with pain.

'True,' he said with steely determination, 'But not for the want of trying. On my part at least.'

'I meant, there are no guarantees . . . ' Elly trailed off, attempting to compensate for her loose tongue without actually apologising. 'What went wrong?' she asked gently.

'Crossed wires, I guess.' He shrugged. 'I assumed Joanne wanted a family like I did. We met at university and married on graduation. Later, she became a flight attendant. Away a lot.' He gazed into the distance at a point somewhere over her right shoulder. 'We always planned to discuss it later, but later never came. Jo volunteered for overseas flights and her absences grew longer until we drifted apart.'

'You must have felt disappointed,' she said softly.

Raw hurt crossed his face. 'And a failure.'

Elly offered a faint smile of encouragement. 'But you survived.'

'Yeah. Took a while though.' He ran his hand over his face in a weary gesture then scowled. 'Next time, I'll get it right.'

4

Elly admired his positive attitude after having his heart broken. 'How can you be sure?'

He looked across at her steadily. 'It's worth trying. Judging by my parents, with the right person, love and communication, marriage can be a highly satisfying partnership.'

'You'd be setting yourself up for heartbreak again,' Elly suggested.

Rusty shrugged. 'Possibly, but I like the idea of coming home to my wife and not turning the key in the lock of an empty house.'

'What if she wasn't there?' Elly posed quietly.

'I'd hope she would be. A full-time mother makes for a solid family unit and stability for the children.'

'I hope you find a woman who shares your dream. These days both partners often work.'

'No shame in setting the bar up high.'

'Of course not.' Elly suffered a moment of despondency that she did not share his expectations and wondered why.

'I wouldn't want second best for my own family.'

No, Elly silently agreed, witnessing the fierce glitter of passion in his eyes. And they won't get it. They'll have the best.

She stared at him. Rusty Webster was an unusual man. He aspired to traditional values and dreams and sought everything she avoided.

Pleasantly weary and choosing not to dwell on their differences, she uncurled her feet and made to stand. But her left foot, tucked beneath her, had grown numb with pins and needles, and gave way. She lurched forward, knocking her shins against the hard edges of the glass-topped table.

She winced and stumbled. From the corner of her eye, Elly saw Rusty leap to his feet and grasp her by the shoulders. Safely steadied, his big hands circled her upper arms and radiated warmth through her shirt. Elly found herself looking him so closely in the face, their noses and mouths almost touched. Almost. Her world stopped and her breath ceased.

'You OK?' His murmured drawl emerged barely above a whisper, his deep raspy voice filled with concern.

She could only nod in response.

'You've hurt your leg.'

He looked down and she felt his hand skimming over her bare flesh, searching for any potential injury. She flinched when his gentle fingers found a bruise.

'I'm fine,' she retorted, gathering her composure and wrenching herself from his hold, appalled by the crazy emotions she felt at his touch. Close up, Rusty Webster was desirable. And marked out for a much more suitable woman.

Rusty eyed her strangely. 'I'll clear the tray and turn off the lights.'

Elly cleared her throat and straightened, flexing her leg. 'I'll go check on Molly before bed.'

He hooked his hands into his jeans at the waist and nodded, but his ardent gaze told her he'd felt a spark of something too. This was not wise. Elly squashed her attraction. He was only passing through and their lives were headed in different directions. Caught up in the moment, they'd passed. It wouldn't happen again.

'See you in the morning.'

Elly buried her agitation and limped across the room, relieved when she was out of sight and within the sanctuary of her bedroom suite. She had just closed the door safely behind her when she remembered. She'd forgotten to check on Molly.

Annoyed that Rusty had distracted her so much that it slipped her mind, she hobbled along to the nursery hoping she didn't encounter him again.

Standing at the cot, Elly gazed down in awe at the still-sleeping placid pink face of contentment, the small body pushing up the bedclothes in a gentle hump.

As she peered at the baby in the soft glow of a dim night-light, her roller coaster heartbeat gradually slowed. Webster had caught her off guard. He'd been so close and his touch had stirred up her dormant hormones. If only she hadn't tripped. Wretched leg, she rubbed it in sympathy.

Just when she had her poise under control, Elly heard movement behind her. Every muscle in her body tensed as Rusty moved up beside her, Elly edged away. 'She's settled.'

'It's her first night in a strange place. If she wakes, I'll give her a bottle. I'll try not to wake you.'

'I won't mind.' Elly's brow dipped into a frown. 'Not having time to care for Molly doesn't mean I don't care. How heartless do you think I am?'

Rusty's jaw clenched and a dark scowl wrinkled his brows. 'I don't think you're heartless at all, Ms George. Good night.'

He turned and left as quietly as he'd come. Elly's shoulders drooped. She couldn't win. No matter what she did, she fell short it seemed.

Next morning, Elly woke and rose early. She telephoned the hospital from her room to check on Rachel's condition. Cheered by the information that her friend had rested well overnight, Elly decided to take Molly to visit her mother after work.

She changed out of her blue silk pyjamas into sports shorts and a crop top, then piled up her thick bouncy hair and snapped a large butterfly clip over it to secure it in place. Neither Rusty nor Molly had stirred in the apartment yet as she crossed to the utilities room and turned on the treadmill.

She switched the treadmill faster, setting up a punishing rhythm. Not fifteen minutes later, Rusty opened the door she had left slightly ajar. Feeling sweaty and self conscious, she cringed with embarrassment when he appeared.

She swallowed hard against the sight of him, sleepy and rumpled and yawning in checked pyjamas and a tight grey T-shirt that hugged his brawny chest. His hands ruffled his sleep-mussed hair, making him look cuddly and enticing, and one incredibly masculine package.

And that was the problem. Elly glanced away and kept pounding. It was becoming increasingly difficult thinking of Rusty as an employee instead of as a highly attractive man.

'Morning.'

She nodded politely and looked straight ahead out of the window.

She sensed his attention on her for too long before he said, 'Great view.'

'It was worth every extra cent I paid for it.'

'I meant inside the apartment.'

Elly's thoughts froze even as her sneakers thumped the moving mat beneath her feet. Flattering, and good for a girl's ego, but she'd need to set him straight. 'That's an inappropriate comment.'

'But true.'

'All the same, as your employer I

could accuse you of inappropriate behaviour for that remark.'

'You certainly could.' He crossed his arms and ankles and leaned a big shoulder against the door jamb. 'But you won't.'

An employee shouldn't look so smug. 'Only because I know you're teasing me.'

She changed the subject. 'Is Molly awake?'

He chuckled. 'All smiles and cute as a button. Come and see what you're missing while I make breakfast.'

'Thanks all the same, but I only kick-start myself with coffee.'

'Don't be like that.' He pushed himself away from the door and scowled. 'Finish your workout, get showered and join us. You're not leaving for work until you've had more than coffee.'

Elly despaired that she would ever be strong enough to resist his irreverent larrikin appeal. 'Yes, Nanny,' she mocked.

After he left, she strode out harder

and longer than usual to work off her frustration of restless discontent.

Refreshingly showered, hair blow-dried and gleaming, Elly stood in her walk-in robe surveying the line of designer suits that filled her closet.

This morning she chose teal, the snug skirt exposing her knees, the first large gold button secured just enough above her cleavage to be decent. She applied make-up and gave her hair a final brush, then bundled up her briefcase and its necessary contents for the day, gave herself a last look in the robe mirror, decided she passed, and went to join Molly and her nanny for breakfast.

She dumped her bag and briefcase on a sofa in the living-room. As she entered the kitchen, Rusty looked up and a flicker of appreciation settled over her stylish appearance.

He always made her feel too feminine. Around him she always felt far too vulnerable and unsure. Well, she'd survived the past twenty-four hours. Taken one day at a time, surely she could manage another week?

He, on the other hand, puddled comfortably around her kitchen looking very appealing and casual in his crumpled pyjamas and uncombed hair.

Elly pulled her concentration into line, focused on Molly and planted a gentle kiss on the top of her soft downy hair, 'Morning, sweetie.'

The child delivered the gift of a messy, but adorable smile as Rusty tied on a bib, sat astride a dining-room chair backwards and started feeding her baby cereal.

Molly's short legs kicked with delight and chuckles of joy erupted every time he pretended to be an aeroplane and zoomed another teaspoonful into her mouth.

'Where did the high chair come from?'

'The apartment manager yesterday.'

Elly shook her head. 'That man can find anything from anywhere at a moment's notice. He's a marvel.'

The strong smell of freshly-brewed coffee besieged her senses and she followed the enticing aroma across the kitchen to pour a cup. She leaned back against the kitchen bench to drink it, noting the boxes of cereal, toast, half empty container of milk and baby bottles littering the counter in an untidy but homely mess.

'There's cereal and fruit on the table, and I can make toast, eggs or pancakes. Whatever you prefer.'

'Breakfast's not a meal. It's a snack,' she argued, lifting her coffee mug in salute. 'This will be fine.'

'You can spare ten minutes,' he growled.

Judging by his firm tone of voice, Elly realised he meant it. He finished feeding Molly, wiped the child's face and fingers then set her down on a play mat.

Molly stared up at him, wide-eyed and unblinking, utterly adoring. Elly knew how the child felt.

'Now, what's it going to be?'

'Oh, really,' she protested.

'At least try some fruit and toast. Peaches and strawberries, with a spread of marmalade on wholemeal to follow?'

She heaved out a sigh of long suffering. 'Since you insist.'

Elly watched him prepare the fruit and accepted the bowl he offered when he finished. As she forked up the chilled slices and stood backed up against the kitchen counter, she had to admit it was a tasty change from the hastily drunk caffeine fix she made do with until she grabbed a pastry with coffee halfway through her morning. If she found time. Sometimes she went hungry till lunch.

The tangy marmalade exploded over the taste buds in her mouth and she had eaten the whole slice of toast before she realised it. Somehow with Rusty and Molly in residence, Elly's usual urgency dwindled.

While his bowl of Weetbix and milk heated in the microwave, he grinned at Elly licking crumbs from her sticky fingers. 'Now, that wasn't so bad after all, was it?'

'Didn't hurt a bit,' she was forced to confess, enjoying the extra few minutes he had forced her to take. 'By the way,' she suddenly remembered, 'I phoned the hospital and Rachel's all right for visitors as from today.'

Her mobile phone rang before she could finish and she strode into the living-room to answer it. 'Hi, Dallas.' She listened and groaned. 'So soon?' She nodded. 'OK, I'll be right in.'

Elly flipped off her phone and smiled down at Molly as the baby gurgled up at her, then turned to Rusty lounging in the kitchen doorway.

'Emergency?'

She crinkled her brows. 'No, but my first appointment is way early. Seems to be the tone of the week.' She grabbed her briefcase, hitched her bag over a shoulder and blew Molly a kiss. 'See you tonight.'

As she dashed for the elevator, the thought hit Elly that tonight seemed an eternity away. She felt disappointed to be missing all the activity in her apartment while she was gone.

The office was crazy all day. Elly had an unscheduled teleconference with the Canberra delegation to clarify points from yesterday's meeting.

By late afternoon, a mountain of paperwork still waited, but she wanted to take Molly to see Rachel in hospital. She crammed all the unfinished mail into her briefcase, deciding to answer emails from her laptop and dictate other notes to Dallas tonight at home.

Her assistant gaped when she revealed her intentions. 'But it's not even five yet. You never leave early.'

'Well, I am today.'

Dallas frowned of concern. 'No problems at home? Molly OK?'

Elly nodded and continued signing the small pile of mail.

'And the nanny?' Her pointed question was loaded with unvoiced innuendo.

Elly rolled her eyes to the ceiling and held back a smile. 'He's proving competent.'

'Be a new experience for you having a man around the house, huh?'

'Dallas, he's an employee,' she insisted.

'Well, I guess in your case any man is better than no man,' Dallas chuckled as she scooped up the pile of signed correspondence and strode across the room, closing the door smartly behind her before her boss had a chance to respond.

What was the big deal about dating and marriage anyway? Elly reflected. It wasn't mandatory in life. Plenty of people remained single and she planned to be one of them. She wasn't born to be a mother.

Hauling her heavy briefcase off the desk, Elly breezed past Dallas at reception with a cheery smile and an awkward wave as she juggled her belongings, and a quick, 'See you tomorrow.'

5

Elly checked the car clock as she inched across Princes Bridge over the Yarra River in thick traffic toward her apartment, hoping there was still time for a hospital visit before Molly's bedtime. Rachel needed to see her daughter. As she hurried into the apartment later, Rusty glanced up, wearing tight jeans and a black polo shirt, he looked dynamic and threatening.

His dark eyes doubled in surprise and his brows twitched higher.

'I know. I'm early.' Elly was relieved to see Molly playing happily on the floor and looking bright. 'Hello sweetheart.' The baby gooed up at her and dribbled.

She unloaded her office bags on a sofa, kicked off her shoes and crouched down beside the child. She would enjoy reuniting mother and daughter again.

'Did she manage a nap today?'

'Sure did. She was tuckered out after our excursion this afternoon.'

Elly was pleased to hear he had taken advantage of the improving spring weather. 'Did you go across to the Botanic Gardens?'

'No. I took Molly to visit her mother in hospital.'

Elly's body and spirits sank, and she groaned. Rachel was a hands-on mother who only billeted Molly into day care in an emergency. 'You didn't!' She sprang to her feet.

Rusty frowned, puzzled. 'I thought that's what you wanted when you mentioned it this morning. I didn't expect you could take her yourself.'

Elly suffered a flash of guilt. 'Exactly my plan. That's why I'm home early.' Exasperated, she paced, voicing her frustrated thoughts. 'I meant to tell you this morning, but when Dallas phoned, I was rushed and forgot.'

'Tell me what?'

Elly swung around to confront him. 'Not to visit Rachel until I'd seen her first.'

Rusty eyed her steadily for a moment. 'Because she didn't know about me?'

She nodded. 'I wanted to explain why I'd hired you.'

'She wasn't concerned. She was ecstatic to see Molly,' Rusty tried to reassure her.

Elly shook her head. 'You don't understand. Rachel's the ultimate natural mother. Even when she was abandoned by Molly's father and left to raise the child alone, she glowed all through pregnancy. She was absolutely rapt about the prospect of having a baby. Molly's the one good thing in her life. Everything centres around that child.'

Elly looked away from Rusty. 'I don't want Rachel to think I've put my business first and only fitted Molly in around the edges. Within hours of the accident, I knew I couldn't devote all the time to Molly that she obviously needed and deserved, and run a business. I had to arrange quality personal care here at home.'

Rusty moved up beside her and she felt the gentle comfort of his hand on her arm. 'Finished persecuting yourself?' His soft voice sounded amused. 'Rachel's fine with the situation. Positive. We introduced ourselves and she played with Molly on her bed for over an hour.'

Elly sighed, feeling miserable. 'I still need to go in and explain.'

'I've already done that.'

'Well, it should have been me because it's my responsibility.'

'Under what law is that exactly?' He chuckled. 'Your spare time's running on empty. Accept a helping hand,' he hinted good naturedly. 'You've had a long day. How about dinner?'

'No, I need to ease my mind first.' Elly frowned, gnawed with distraction and worry. 'Just save me something on a plate. I'll heat it up later and eat while I work.'

'It won't be a problem. Rachel understands. We talked.'

Elly was still wracked with guilt as she drove toward the Alfred Hospital. In Rachel's room, her friend reclined against a stack of pillows, her brown curly hair sprawled about her, watching television, attached to a drip and monitors, blessed with a natural radiance that seemed to have been enhanced since motherhood. The instant she glimpsed Elly hovering in the doorway, her nut brown eyes sparked into life.

'Come and sit down.' She patted the bed. 'You must be exhausted. And here I've been lounging in bed all day.' She grinned.

Elly hugged her, careful not to squeeze too tight in case it hurt somewhere. 'With good reason.' Elly settled beside her. 'You're looking so much better.'

Rachel waved a dismissive arm. 'Doctors all said I was lucky. It was worse than it looked.' She picked up Elly's hand and gave it a quick squeeze, wincing with the effort. 'Thanks for coming to my rescue with Molly. You've always been there for me.'

Elly took a deep breath and expressed what was on her mind. 'You don't mind that I hired a nanny to look after Molly while I'm at work, do you?'

Rachel shook her head. 'Goodness, no. I suspected you didn't know what you were in for when you offered, but I was too miserable to explain. I know your business is important. I'm just grateful Molly's fine and in top care.'

'Really? I hadn't been back to my apartment thirty minutes and I knew I was in trouble,' Elly confessed. 'I'm not cut out to be a mother.'

'Fiddlesticks. You'd soon get the hang of it. Motherhood doesn't always come as naturally as people think.'

Elly finally relaxed. Rusty was right after all. Even though her stomach rumbled with hunger and she was bone weary, she settled down to spend time with her friend.

'Rusty hardly seems like a nanny,'

Rachel said. 'He's such a natural with kids.' In a lowered voice, she added, 'Is he gorgeous or what? And that hair? Don't you just want to run your hands in it?'

A rush of embarrassed heat flooded through Elly. She'd thought exactly the same herself. 'He's certainly experienced with children.'

'And he's living in.' Rachel flicked her a teasing grin. 'That's a bonus.'

'Well, obviously it's more convenient that way.' Elly grew defensive.

'Emmanuelle George.' Rachel nudged her friend's arm. 'You're embarrassed. How many people know?'

'You and Dallas. And if you breathe a word, you're out of my will, OK?'

Rachel shook with suppressed laughter, groaning in discomfort. 'How many times have I heard that before? Time you had a little action in your life.'

'Rusty Webster is not action,' Elly protested too readily.

'Whatever you say.' She grinned. 'But

it's about time you slowed up and smelt the roses.'

'My business is my life.'

'Fiddlesticks.' Rachel winced as she moved position. 'You've been using that excuse for years. Maybe this time romance has found you instead of you having to go out and find it.'

'Oh, tosh.' Elly flashed her a warning glare. 'Aren't you too sick to be giving advice?' she muttered, feeling uncomfortable.

'Never felt better.' But her mouth turned down a little at the edges. 'Except I miss Molly. I can't wait to get out of here.'

A nurse appeared, checked Rachel's equipment and chart, and suggested the patient needed rest.

'I promise I'll visit every day.' Elly rose, kissed her friend on the cheek and left.

By the time the penthouse elevator doors slid apart, Elly was beyond tired and past feeling hungry. She just wanted sleep. Impossible, of course, because hours of work lurked in her briefcase. She trudged to her front door, unenthusiastic for once at the thought of working late.

The moment she stepped into her apartment, Elly's homecoming was rewarded by the sound of Rusty's deep low voice and Molly's gurgling chuckles. She smiled. Home. It sure felt good tonight.

In the living-room, Rusty was swinging Molly high into the air, the reason for the child's helpless laughter. Elly's cares fell away at the happy sight and it occurred to her that she had just entered another world, but she pushed them aside.

Rusty didn't turn around at her approach. Instead, he whispered to Molly, 'Aunt Elly's home.'

The child's eyes lit up and her tiny mouth opened into an angelic smile.

Elly joined them. 'I can't believe she's still awake.'

Rusty glanced across at her and smiled. 'She had such a long sleep this afternoon, I'm working on the eventual exhaustion theory.' Even as he spoke, Molly rubbed her eyes and grizzled. 'Jackpot. Bottle and bedtime, I'd say.'

'I know how she feels.' Elly massaged her neck and stretched to keep her weary joints limber.

'You look beat.' He set Molly down on the floor and gathered up her scattered toys. 'How about you give Molly her supper?'

'Oh, no,' she said hastily, recoiling at the thought, not keen to showcase her inept motherhood skills in front of him. 'That's all right. You do it.'

Rusty darted her a challenging glance. 'Molly's missed you. She'd love it.' Without giving her time to object, he added, 'I bet Rachel was pleased to see you.'

Deftly sidetracked, Elly agreed. 'Yes. She's recovering well.' She struggled with the words. 'You were right, of course. She was impressed with you and didn't mind my arranging for help with Molly at all.'

As they looked at each other, a flare of understanding passed between them. To his credit, Rusty didn't actually say, I told you so.

Elly turned and headed for her room. 'Back in five. I'll change before I feed Molly.'

She undressed and pulled out her favourite pair of snug-fitting stretch jeans and a comfortable shirt, determined to be herself, more accustomed to Rusty now.

She padded barefoot back into the living-room. Rusty emerged from the kitchen carrying Molly and a bottle of milk. He rolled an approving gaze over her and an awareness of his survey curled through her stomach.

He transferred the baby into her arms and held out the bottle. Molly's softness and warmth seeped against her, subtle baby smells drifting across her senses and into her subconscious.

Rusty scooted about the living-room floor packing up toys, then disappeared, tactfully leaving them alone, for which

Elly was grateful.

She settled back into one of her soft plump sofas and nudged the teat into the child's mouth. Ironic that she would rather run a company than handle an eight-month-old-baby.

As the baby drank and her small fingers wrapped around the bottle, Elly was awed by how much she looked like Rachel with the promise of dark hair. She smelled fresh and sweet. Totally captivated by the small soul in her lap, the real world faded from Elly's awareness and her attention focused wholly on the child in her arms.

Molly blinked up at her, wide-eyed as she slurped and dribbled on her night-time feed. Deep within Elly, a bond of affection surged into life. Holding and feeding Molly Jean Golding raised unfamiliar and protective stirrings, and Elly knew she would guard the sleepy child with her life.

By the time the bottle was empty, Molly drowsily yawned and Elly was completed relaxed, distanced from the day's responsibilities but starving. Whatever Rusty had prepared, she would demolish it.

Handling Molly gently, Elly carried her into the nursery.

'All done?' Rusty fussed about the room, unnecessary since it was always neat.

With his guidance, Elly changed Molly and laid her in the cot. Rusty pulled up the covers and the baby was asleep before they left the room.

'Time to eat,' he said over his shoulder as they made for the kitchen.

'My thoughts exactly. I'm ravenous. What's for dinner?'

'Spinach fettuccine in a carbonara sauce.'

Elly wasn't sure she'd heard right and drooled. Pasta. Her favourite. 'Lead me to it.'

He spooned out a serving into a bowl and heated it in the microwave. 'Did you get your report finished?' she asked.

He nodded. 'E-mailed it off this morning.'

The microwave beeped, Rusty retrieved the bowl and Elly found herself a fork.

As she popped a creamy prawn into her mouth, Rusty scowled. 'You're not going to eat that standing up, are you? It's bad for the digestion.'

'OK,' she muttered in good humour. 'I'll sit.'

They moved back into the living-room and assumed seats on opposite couches. Elly sank into the soft leather and continued eating.

Rusty sat forward on the edge of his sofa, elbows resting on his knees, hands clasped between them. 'How much work do you have in that briefcase tonight?'

Drawn to hold his gaze, as she always seemed inclined, beckoned by the dusky colour of his eyes and some other indefinable enticement, she groaned. 'Too much.'

'Urgent?'

'Some of it.'

He paused. 'Can you delegate or leave some of it until tomorrow?'

Elly twirled the pasta around her fork and savoured another mouthful before responding, contemplating his mental nudge, finding it strange discussing work with anyone other than Dallas and even stranger that anyone should be interested. 'Guess I could.'

'Ah, but will you?'

Elly smiled to herself and muttered. 'Point taken. All work and no play etcetera.'

'Weekend's coming up. I hope you plan to spend some of it outdoors.'

'Depends.' If she finished reading those agreements before running them by her lawyers next week.

'No excuses,' he insisted with lazy assurance. 'Molly and I have an outing in mind to make sure you do.'

'I'll be fine. Working seven days is my life. You just concentrate on caring for Molly.'

'It's a pleasure looking after both of you.'

More than mildly disturbed by the powerful way he looked at her and the confusion it caused in the pit of her stomach, Elly eased toward a less personal topic.

'Next project I'm working on is in the MacDonnell Ranges about an hour east of the Alice in the Territory.'

'Do you work mainly from home at Badger Creek?'

'It's my base.'

'What's it like?' It sounded rough and isolated.

'A house in the bush near a national park. Mud bricks which I made myself. Great insulation. Lots of stained glass. Rosellas, lorikeets and kookaburras perched out on the balcony railing or on the birdfeeders. A big open fireplace that heats the whole house.'

His description only emphasised another chasm in the differences between them. It sounded positively Arcadian yet she heard the passion in Rusty's voice and conceded to herself it sounded interesting. Exactly the kind of place he would choose to live, of course.

'You're welcome to come out and visit any time.' His sincere invitation was unexpected.

'Thank you.' Her voice grew husky. Dragging her eyes away to avoid the confusion raiding her brain, she cleared her throat. 'I'll keep it in mind if I'm ever out that way.' Elly knew her indifference sounded impolite but she couldn't encourage any interest no matter how much attraction she felt.

'Consider the offer always open,' he drawled.

His proposition suggested keeping in touch after his job was finished. She wondered why when he knew their work and lifestyles clashed.

Feeling awkward and weary, Elly rose and started for the kitchen. 'Well, work calls.'

Rusty was on his feet facing her and rescued the bowl from her grasp. 'I'll get that.'

His warm flesh brushed hers and first Elly's arm, then her entire body, flushed with heat. She snatched away her hand

and tucked it safely into the pocket of her jeans. Startled by the electricity arcing between them, Elly unconsciously held her breath, appalled to feel such an intense reaction when Rusty Webster was not her type.

Mesmerised, Elly discovered her feet anchored to the carpet. Her toes curled with tension, not helped by Rusty's gaze hovering on her mouth. He seemed on the verge of making a pass and her heart pounded with the possibility. Then Rusty blinked and ground his jaw, stepped back, creating distance, and the moment ended.

His eyes lingered over her a while longer, making her feel helpless and trapped. 'Don't stay up working too late,' he murmured.

Work, Elly suddenly remembered, managed a weak smile and scrambled for her office.

Once inside, she slammed the door and leant against it, breathing hard. She'd seen the hungry look in Rusty's eyes.

Bottom line, an attraction existed between them. Understandable living under the same roof. Rusty Webster was a handsome man with a humming energy about him she found exciting. Her wisest move was not to let it happen again. Distance. That was the key and, in order to achieve it, she devised a plan.

6

Late into the night, Elly struggled to concentrate. Only half-finishing her mountain of work, she set the alarm for five and crawled into bed.

Next morning, she'd worked, exercised, showered and dressed before Rusty and Molly stirred. Her avoidance strategy worked and she slipped out of the apartment, leaving a note.

The plan succeeded all week although Elly had trouble thinking of it that way. Practising her separation theory was tough. It took scheduling and indifference. She rarely saw Molly and when she connected with Rusty, conversation was courteous and brief.

Once — was it only a week ago? — she had been content with work. Now she found she missed his company. Which only made their tense situation worse. Like a brewing thunderstorm, Elly endured his side glances and reserve knowing, as the weekend approached, and two whole days together looked ahead, new arrangements would need to be contrived.

By Friday night, work had piled up in the agency and Elly left way late. With hospital visiting hours long past, she phoned Rachel instead, promising a longer visit at the weekend.

As Elly drove along Collins Street, the city's grand boulevard and precinct of serious money, she mulled over a solution. Passing the leafy plane trees with their beautiful fairy lights twinkling among the branches, she hit on a brilliant flash of inspiration that would take care of tomorrow.

She breezed into the apartment as casually as she could muster, her nerves stretched as tight as an elastic band.

'Rusty? Molly?' Elly strode between rooms, opening doors and peering in, but the apartment was silent and empty. Her tension was replaced by an eerie apprehension. She grabbed the phone and called Rusty's mobile.

'Rusty Webster.'

'I'm home. Where are you?' she demanded.

'You didn't see my note in the kitchen?' he replied curtly.

Annoyed, Elly marched back through the apartment and noticed the scrap of paper propped up against a coffee mug on the counter. She scanned his scrawly handwriting and gaped. 'What on earth are you doing on the roof at this time of night?'

'Playing. In case you hadn't noticed, it's a beautiful night.' She hadn't. 'Do you need us?'

Elly winced at his blunt retort and her heart lurched with a hurtful ache. 'I need to talk to you.' She paused. 'I'll come up.'

From the end of the outer hall, Elly climbed the short flight of stairs to her private rooftop garden, a penthouse perk she rarely used. She emerged from the top step into the evening air, tilting up her gaze. The moon was huge and full, a watery golden circle, and with such a glittering magical spread of city lights, who needed stars?

Shielded from any breeze by the waist-high stucco walls, Molly played happily on a thick padded play mat. Rusty sat at the wrought iron outdoor table working at his laptop, head bent in concentration, the slightest current of air ruffling the wave of hair trailing across his nape. The light from his computer screen reflected his ominous unsmiling profile.

Running circles all week avoiding him didn't prepare her for the power of his presence. She struggled to begin conversation. Molly solved her dilemma by catching sight of her, pointing a small finger and chortling.

'Hey, baby.'

She crossed to the child, bent down and scooped her into her arms, planting a spontaneous kiss on her cheek. Molly snuggled into her neck and Elly glowed with warmth. When she dared glance at

Rusty, she saw a duet of pleasure and pain on his face, realising he suffered all she felt and more. They couldn't give in.

He collapsed his laptop lid, pushed back his chair with a scrape and, in one slow motion movement, rose to his feet.

Unshaven and scowling, hands planted on his hips, he said, 'You're still alive, I see.'

Elly shrank from his black expression and harsh words, even as she melted at the brawny sight of him. All the more reason to stay apart. She'd been dreading this moment all week and forced indifference with a shrug. 'It's been a busy week. That's the reason I hired you in the first place.'

'Of course.' His tone was clipped. 'You have something you want to discuss?' he prompted.

Molly stuck a finger in Elly's mouth. Caught off guard, she burst out laughing and removed it. She glanced back to Rusty to find him looking at her with a strange intensity.

'Yes. You're due some time off. I thought you might appreciate having tomorrow free for the football.'

He pulled a tight smile. 'That's very thoughtful of you. There's nothing for me here.' His cutting barb and faraway gaze tugged at her insides as though she'd landed him in a physical blow. 'I look forward to it. Beer and hot dogs. What more could a man want?'

He sank his hands into his pockets, glaring, assessing. A chill breeze stirred the air around them and Elly shivered. 'We should take Molly downstairs.' She cuddled the child in her arms and edged toward them.

'I'll pack up here and follow you down.'

Rusty watched Elly bobbing down the steps carrying Molly. He admired all the qualities he shouldn't. The soft hair he ached to touch. The way it always swung just above her shoulders when she walked with purpose, as now. The curvy figure in slim fitting trousers.

She trapped his full attention whenever she was around. Which hadn't been much this past week. And they both knew why. She was scared, and it wrenched his insides. Just when he found a woman again that stirred his interest, she faked disinterest. But he'd seen those soft blue eyes sparkle with light when he looked at her.

He figured her reserve was his nanny thing. Well, he wouldn't always be an employee and any supposed ethics could be tossed out the window. Then he'd see how the cool Elly George responded.

Sure, they were different. He lived in the bush. She was a city woman, ran a big company and worked too many hours a day to make it happen. She didn't want marriage. He did and wanted a bunch of kids to go with it.

But he never paid attention to limitations and thrived on challenges. Plain truth was, he wanted to get to know Elly George better.

By the time he returned downstairs,

he'd decided to ditch caution and opt for a little excitement, deciding Elly George was well worth giving it a shot. He had nothing to lose except his pride. He'd lost that before and gotten over it. This time, though, wiser, he'd sort out any issues up front.

★ ★ ★

Elly opened one eye to find sunshine streaming across her bed and the clock revealing she had overslept. She sprang up and moaned. 'I'm supposed to be minding Molly today.'

She threw a silk robe over her pyjama trousers and padded from the bedroom wing. A peep into the nursery revealed an empty cot. Still sleepy, she shuffled into the living-room, spellbound at the sight. Positioned near the full length windows and flooded with brilliant morning light, Rusty sat astride a chair, wearing his black and yellow football gear. A sweater over his jeans, scarf flung about his neck and peaked cap worn backwards.

Molly faced him in her high chair, eyes wide, face animated with delight. With one hand, he dipped a small plastic ring into a bottle, raised it in the air and blew bubbles. With the other, while Molly reached out trying to catch them, he deftly spooned another mouthful of baby cereal into her mouth.

Elly melted. How did a bloke so manfully dressed, ready for a game of Aussie Rules football and feeding a baby, manage to look so seriously attractive? The sooner he left the better.

Combing desperate fingers through her ruffled hair, she headed towards them. 'Today's supposed to be your day off,' she said lightly.

'Aunt Elly's awake,' he said to Molly without turning around.

Elly squirmed with guilt. 'I meant to set my alarm — '

'No bother. That's what I'm here for, remember?' He darted back. 'I'm nearly finished here. When I do, she's all yours.'

Awkwardly, she half-raised an arm. 'I'll go shower then.'

She bolted back to her suite. Well, at least they were talking. By the time she returned, Molly was fed and happily playing on the living-room floor, the kitchen was spotless and Rusty prowled the apartment. A plump backpack was ready to go on a sofa.

His gaze flickered over her short denim skirt and tee shirt then hovered on her mouth until Elly felt as if she couldn't breathe.

'Any concerns about Molly while I'm away?'

Elly shook her head. 'No.'

'You're going to see Rachel?'

'Yes.'

'Then I'll need your car keys so I can transfer the car seat.'

While he was gone, Elly breathed a sigh of relief. She turned to Molly in the middle of the room. 'Well, sweetie, soon it will be just you and me. It'll be a new experience having Aunt Elly take care of you for a change, won't it?'

She filled a bowl with cereal, watching Molly while she ate, undaunted at childminding alone for the day. She was spreading toast in the kitchen when Rusty returned. He set the keys on the counter and leant back against it, arms folded, legs crossed at the ankles. She realised her mistake when she glanced over at him, a breath away. Captivated, she stared.

This close, Elly smelt his freshness, stirred by his raw casual appeal, reassured by his quiet reliable presence yet resentful he wasn't more her type.

Suddenly Rusty was snapping his fingers before her eyes and grinning. 'You've left me again.'

Elly refocused to discover marmalade over her fingers instead of the toast, and licked it off. 'Pardon?'

'I said, I'll be off then.' He checked his wrist watch. 'I've arranged to meet my dad and brother-in-law, Steve.'

'Boys' day out.' She forced a smile. Amazing. Unlike her family, the Websters actually enjoyed being together.

Rusty pushed himself away from the counter and crossed the kitchen, hesitating in the doorway. 'Say hi to Rachel for me. She must be due out this week?'

Elly nodded. 'We'll know more after we visit today.'

'Catch you tonight. I should be back by six.'

'No rush. Have a great day.' She nibbled her toast and tried to appear composed as he sauntered into the lounge.

'You be good for Aunt Elly today, Possum, OK?' He gently tousled Molly's raven curls then rose. 'See you girls tonight.' He shrugged on his backpack, sent them both a devastating smile and a wave, and was gone.

The apartment fell silent. Molly stared at the door as though expecting him to return, her mouth turned down at the edges. Elly gave up on the toast because it tasted like cardboard in her mouth and rescued her goddaughter, diverting her attention with blocks.

Before Molly grew too tired, Elly changed and dressed her, then headed for the hospital. In Rachel's room on the fourth floor, the delighted mother smothered her daughter with sloppy kisses and cuddles.

'Hello, precious,' Rachel cooed. 'Gosh, I've missed you and I only saw you yesterday.'

The rapture on the faces of reunited mother and child wrenched Elly's heart with envy. 'So, when do they set you free?' she asked, trying to sound bright.

'They still haven't given me a definite date,' she sighed.

'Well, it can't be much longer. You're looking great and remarkably mobile considering what you suffered a week ago.'

Selfishly, Elly reflected on the shrinking number of days until Rusty and Molly left. Seeing her friend's wistful face, she grew ashamed.

'What's Rusty doing today?' Rachel asked as if reading her thoughts.

'Football. He's a big Tigers fan.' She rolled her eyes. 'You should have seen what he was wearing when he left the apartment.'

'All the gear, huh? Guess you've grown used to having him around,' she probed.

Elly remained evasive. 'He's been great with Molly.'

'He mentioned he was divorced.' Rachel scoffed. 'What female in her right mind would ditch a guy like that? He's every woman's dream.'

Too soon, Molly grew irritable, squirming in Rachel's lap. 'OK, precious, we get the message,' she released her daughter.

'We'll all come in tomorrow.' Elly lifted Molly from Rachel's arms. 'You might know your release date by then.'

Back at the apartment, while Molly napped, Elly tried reducing her load of paperwork. She flipped files, leafed idly through pages and made notes, but procrastinated.

Instead, she ambled into the living-room and reached for the television remote. Selecting the sports channel, Elly couldn't believe she was actually watching football. She never followed sports.

Oops. Rusty's team was losing and it was only half time.

7

Elly's heart curled with pleasure later when she heard the spare key in the front door. Rusty was back. Windblown and tousled, untidily appealing, she cringed with regret knowing she had missed him.

His sweater was tied around his waist over a Tigers T-shirt; a loaf of pane di casa wrapped in crisp bakery paper escaped the top of his backpack and smelt heavenly.

Elly's stomach churned with excitement and apprehension at his killer smile of welcome. 'Sorry your team lost,' she blurted out when he was barely in the door and bit her tongue at the lapse.

Smugly, he teased, 'You heard the results?'

'Um . . . I saw it on television.'

His eyes danced. 'You watched the game?'

He looked about to reach out and

grab her with delight. Her heart galloped at the prospect and she froze, but he stopped himself and rubbed his hands together instead.

'I thought you were supposed to be working?' He shrugged off his backpack.

Elly downplayed her interest. 'I just turned it on to see how your team was doing.'

He combed his hands through his messy hair and grimaced. 'Not so good, obviously. I can't believe the goals they missed.'

She indicated the bread. 'Is that dinner?'

'Sure is, and you have a choice. Molly or the kitchen.'

Elly lifted Molly off the floor. 'This one I can handle. What are we having with the bread?'

'Homemade vegetable soup.'

How did he always manage to make the simplest meal sound like a gourmet feast? 'How long do you need?'

He shrugged. 'Forty minutes?'

Elly bathed Molly then she wrapped her up in a thick fluffy towel and carried her back into the nursery where they played as she dried and dressed her ready for bed.

Any wonder the day had frittered away, Elly thought. The smaller the child, the more time they absorbed, but she wouldn't have traded any of it for any paperwork.

'Dinner's ready.' Rusty appeared in the doorway as Elly finished tucking Molly's toes into pink pyjamas and kissed her on the cheek before swinging her up into her arms. 'You seem to be getting the hang of the motherhood thing.' His dark eyes covered her with a steady gaze and her heart leapt at the compliment and the affection in his voice.

'Do you think so?' She felt her skin grow hot.

His expressive dark eyes and easy smile could become addictive. This close, she was powerless to break away.

She moved past him before she did

something foolish like kiss that soft mouth of his. 'I hope you made plenty of soup because I'm starving.'

Seated around the dining table later, Rusty fed a pureed version of the soup to Molly seated in her high chair between them. In between, Elly related the events of her day and their visit to Rachel. Rusty rehashed every kick of the football match, muttering over unfair umpire decisions and his team's loss.

Later, Rusty cleaned up in the kitchen and Elly tried to settle Molly to sleep. Unusually restless, she cuddled the child tight, hummed to her and massaged her back. Soon the little eyelids drooped and her tiny head grew heavy on Elly's shoulder.

Instead of coffee, Rusty brought glasses of shiraz and sank on to the living-room sofa beside her. Rusty angled around, hands crossed on his chest, feet stretched out under the coffee table. 'It's going to be a glorious day tomorrow. Pity to waste it.'

Elly groaned. What on earth did he have in mind? Something heavenly and exactly what she didn't need. 'I have to work,' she reminded him.

'Sure. But you can't work all day.'

'Yes, I can,' she argued.

The image of a cosy threesome filled her mind. Except the child wasn't hers and the man never likely to be. In days, she would resume her solo life again. She caught Rusty's subdued expression as though she'd just sacked him, and softened. Oh, why not take some time off? Wasn't Dallas always spouting the benefits of fresh air and sunshine?

'OK,' she muttered. 'What did you have in mind?'

Her reward was a seriously devastating grin. 'A lazy start to the day, a stroll along the river and brunch.'

It sounded feasible. She could fit in work later. 'All right but just for a while. Can I help with anything?'

Rusty shook his head and murmured, 'I'll organise everything. Just bring yourself.'

'Slow down, Molly will miss the ducks.'

Elly turned back at Rusty's complaint, striding along one step behind her as she pushed the stroller along the meandering botanic gardens pathways. His dark eyes sparkled behind the larrikin smile.

She wrinkled her nose and groaned. 'You talked me out of my treadmill this morning so I'm getting my exercise now. I should be working, you know.'

'You didn't take much convincing.'

True. Her heart and mood had lifted when he suggested it last night. 'Well, I need to walk off those pancakes you cooked for breakfast,' she dredged up another excuse for keeping distance between them.

The balmy spring sunshine seeped into their backs as they strolled by small lakes and ponds, through a cool fern gully and past a broad oak-shaded lawn.

As Elly glanced across at him, she

wondered if she would ever be part of a real family, surprised by the fulfilment he and Molly had introduced into her life this past week.

Elly tugged her gaze away from him to deflect a fresh surge of emotion, alarmed that he always had that effect.

He had been her support this past week, sliding seamlessly into her life. Unbelievable that she had only known him for seven days. A week ago, she'd spent all of her time working. Now she happily ignored it and pushed a baby in a stroller with an attractive divorcee by her side.

His voice entered her senses. 'How about brunch?'

'Great idea. What mysteries do you have in the hamper beside that roast chicken you cooked before we left?'

'Got to your senses, huh?' he drawled.

'Nothing like home cooking. Especially yours.'

'You're just tossing out compliments because you want to be fed.' Rusty chuckled and Elly's chest twisted with longing at the deeply evocative sound. She'd been rash agreeing to this outing today.

He opened the wicker basket stowed in the parcel rack under Molly's stroller and unpacked the contents on to the tartan rug he spread on the grass.

'Finger food.' Elly rubbed her hands together, kneeling down. 'Ideal for a picnic with little Miss Golding here.'

Elly handed a Vegemite crust to Molly who grasped it and automatically put it into her mouth.

She peeled the shell from a soft boiled egg, sprinkled it with salt and pepper. 'I really must learn how to cook.'

'I'd be happy to teach you.'

It wasn't the first time Rusty had hinted at continuing their friendship and her heart tugged with regret knowing their chances of success were slim. 'You'll forget all about me when you leave.'

'Oh, I think your memory is liable to linger for a while.' He flashed her a lazy heart-stopping smile and a wink then cracked open a can of soft drink, poured them each a coloured plastic glassful and handed one to Elly.

'This is the first time I've seen you fully relaxed since we met.'

His brown eyes drew her into their depths until she felt breathless. Elly shrugged off his observation and selected a piece of warm chicken. 'It must be the weekend.'

'It's more than that.'

'Is it? Then maybe it's Molly.' She broke their gaze to look out across the river. 'Truth to tell, I feel guilty about being here.'

'I thought so. Why?' came his soft urge.

She turned back to him with mild irritation. He was deliberately making it difficult. 'You know I have wads of work to do. The nanny is supposed to be a good influence,' she grumbled good-naturedly and sipped her drink.

'You can't tell me you're not enjoying yourself?'

'No, I can't. I've appreciated the break.' She tilted back her face to catch some sun. 'I don't usually take time off even at weekends.'

'You should.'

She caught him staring with a heavy narrowed gaze. Elly turned away to avoid the pull, wishing she didn't find him so appealing. 'I guess I've gotten out of the habit in recent years.'

'Maybe it's time you started some new ones.'

'Maybe it's time you stopped interfering.'

'My interest is genuine.'

'I'm sure it is.' She hesitated, facing him. 'What I don't understand is why.'

He pretended to look crushed. 'You don't?'

She grew irritated, afraid of her feelings. 'No. Is there any point to all this?'

'Everyone deserves a life. Your business is important and a commendable achievement.'

'But?'

Molly spluttered on a mouthful of food, interrupting them. Elly leant across the stroller and wiped her mouth with the bib.

Rusty's voice floated across to her as she performed the task. 'I presume there's more to Elly George than work. I'd like to find out.'

She fidgeted, aware of his implication and murmured, 'Like what?'

'To know more about you. Will the real Elly George please stand up.'

He smiled and it rocked her world. She wanted to crumble at his feet. 'I never like talking about myself,' Elly admitted.

'Am I that much of a threat?'

He was watching her and seeing far more than she wanted. Oh, the agony and ecstasy of that slow and dangerous smile. If he kept gaping at her like that, she'd throw herself into his arms right here and now in full public view.

With Rusty's long legs sprawled out on the rug, the sun glinting off the lighter strands in his dark hair and the wind teasing its edges, no woman with a pulse could resist him. All she could focus on was that great body and tempting mouth.

Elly shook her head. 'With your charm, I don't understand why . . . ' She stopped herself mid-conversation, embarrassed by her slip.

'Why what?' Rusty prompted, eyeing her closely.

She suspected he knew what she had been about to say and hesitated, not wanting to hurt him. 'Why any woman would leave you,' she said carefully.

Eventually he said, 'Neither do I.' The edges of his mouth quirked in amusement. 'I thought I was a reasonable catch.'

Elly pushed out a long slow breath of relief. 'You still are.'

'Reassuring. Remember to include that in my reference when I leave.' Rusty's face shadowed and he looked away from her across the lawns and people, to some abstract place beyond that existed only in his mind. After a while, his attention refocused on her. 'I honestly thought my marriage was for keeps.'

Elly saw the ache backing his gaze and nostalgic regret tugged at her compassion. Marriage and kids were so significant to him, he defied hurt again to achieve it. She felt a coward for not being brave enough to do the same thing.

'I'm sorry you didn't achieve it first time round.'

Rusty faked bravado and made light of his failed marriage. 'I didn't think it was too much to ask.'

'Neither do I. Providing both parties want the same things.'

Arched eyebrows of surprise defined his face. 'I'm surprised to hear you say so.'

Elly's back straightened with purpose. 'Just because I don't see myself ever getting married, doesn't mean I don't see that it works for others.'

'My folks are my role models and

give me hope that one day I can achieve what they have.'

'I'm sure all those sisters will help you,' she teased.

He shook his head. 'If you're thirty and single, you're a prime target. They snoop.'

Elly heard the fondness in his voice and thought it sounded wonderfully interfering. 'It means they care.'

'You don't talk much about your home and family.'

'I don't have as much to tell. Lack of numbers.' She tried not to feel inadequate.

'I'm listening.'

Elly grew nervous. 'What would you like to know?'

'Whatever you want to share.'

She drew in a long breath. 'My parents' house is grand, stone, two storeys. Stunning portico at the front. Circular driveway lined with dozens of white standard roses. Manicured lawns.' Elly shrugged and pulled her mouth into a wry grin. 'I'm sure you get the picture. But I would hardly call it a home.'

'Were you happy?'

She reflected a moment. 'I thought so at the time. I had everything I wanted. If I didn't, all I had to do was ask.'

'But you didn't.'

'How could I? It was clear I had more than most and I've always recognised and appreciated that.'

Molly whimpered, distracting them and Rusty handed her a teething rattle to ease the irritation.

When he returned his attention to Elly again, it was as though his eyes had never left her face. He reached over and squeezed her hand. The simple touch let her know he understood.

'You can share my family if you feel yours falls short,' he offered and his smile melted her heart. 'I can promise you'll never have a dull moment in your life again. But I can also predict you'll never have any privacy either.'

Elly swallowed hard, touched by his

sensitivity, and uttered an unsteady laugh.

Their lunch had moved on to watermelon and strawberries. When Rusty offered Molly some fruit, her tiny mouth opened like a baby bird waiting to be fed. Juice dribbled down her chin and he wiped it off.

When Rusty packed up the food hamper and patted the free space beside him, Elly hesitated. Tempted, she stretched out alongside. Tinkling music from a cruising ice cream van grew louder as it approached along the riverside avenue deeply shaded by spreading old English elms.

Rusty's eyes lit up at the sight of the vehicle. 'Ah, Mr Whippy to the rescue.' He scrambled to his feet and loped over to join the line of children waiting to be served alongside.

Elly grinned to herself. He could be such a boy at heart. She stared after him with greedy indulgence, trying not to make her attention too obvious.

Elly sighed. What had Rusty Webster's ex-wife been thinking? You grabbed a man like that with open arms and kept him for life.

The vision of him striding back toward her, ice creams in hand, stirred longing within her for what could never be. By the time he handed her the soft dessert topped with chocolate and nuts, it was already beginning to melt.

'You have a dob of ice cream about here.' He pointed to the side of her mouth.

'Oh.' Elly's tongue darted out to capture it.

Rusty shook his head and his hair shimmered. 'It's too low,' he murmured.

Elly held her breath as Rusty whipped a tissue from its box — always kept handy with Molly around — and reached out to drift the flimsy material across the corner of her mouth. It almost wasn't a touch at all. More like a whispered caress so that her world as she knew it stopped for the briefest moment until he was done.

8

The tenderness in Rusty's glance and voice was clear. Elly found her attention constantly returning to him like a boomerang to its source.

Needing to break the influence, she said quickly, 'We should head back to go visit Rachel.'

Without waiting for his agreement, she rose and brushed herself down, determined to ignore temptation. A strained silence lingered between them for their return walk through the gardens. Rusty pushed Molly's stroller and Elly developed an intense interest in the scenery to avoid looking at him. Not that she appreciated the towering eucalyptus or the beauty and tranquillity of the ornamental lake because her concentration lay elsewhere.

Back at the apartment, while Rusty attended Molly, Elly changed into jeans and a black shirt. She pulled up the collar, spread ruby gloss across her mouth and stared at herself in the mirror.

But when she joined him in the living-room, her resolve and defences faded. One glimpse of the man again set her pulses racing. She kept remembering the gardens, the way his hair had been messed by the breeze, those gorgeous brown eyes.

'You're doing it again.'

Elly refocused. 'I'm sorry?'

He grinned. 'Daydreaming.'

Elly shrugged. 'My brain's taking the weekend off.'

Rusty chuckled. 'Your mind never stops. And you looked too relaxed for the preoccupation to be work.'

'Well, it was.'

'I find that hard to believe.'

Irritated that he could so accurately read her, Elly scowled, heading for the door. 'Rachel will be waiting.'

They took Rusty's RV to the hospital. The instant the three visitors appeared in Rachel's room, she beamed, glowing with improved health. She perched on the edge of her bed wearing make up, her freshly washed hair gleaming.

'Great news.' Rachel's arms spread wide and her daughter disappeared into a motherly hug. 'I'm being released on Wednesday.'

Elly tried to respond positively to her friend's delight. 'That's fantastic. I know how much you've missed Molly.'

As she would, too, she realised when the child was gone. Not to mention the nanny. Both had enhanced her life's experience. One she treasured and would repeat in a second.

Rusty tactfully hovered in the background, ever the strong quiet presence, leaving the women to plan what Rachel termed her escape mid-week.

'The hospital has arranged home help for a few weeks so everything's been taken care of.'

'I'll come pick you up and drive you back to your flat.'

Rachel's dark brows dipped into a

frown. 'Can you spare the time away from work?'

Elly stifled a twinge of remorse that even her best friend could think her so obsessed with work she didn't have time for them. 'For my best friend? Of course.'

Seeing Molly snuggle against Rachel, Elly's heart warmed. In three days, their separation would begin, one of many partings on that day. They had a date to work with and arrangements to set in motion for Rachel's release. Rusty would move on to his Northern Territory project and Elly could devote full concentration back to her business.

When Rusty's car turned off the street and down into the car park later, Rusty cut the engine and carried Molly toward the elevator. Feeling forsaken, Elly trailed behind.

Up in the apartment, while Rusty fed and bathed his charge before putting her to bed, she gathered up the day's belongings, transferred soiled clothes into the laundry and dropped Molly's toys into her box.

She jumped when Rusty reappeared, too aware of being alone with him for the first time today. He didn't speak but his eyes brimmed with yearning, leaving her exposed and vulnerable. She struggled against the undertow of his gaze and fought for dignity.

'I've reheated leftover soup,' he murmured. 'Hope that's OK for dinner.'

Elly nodded. 'Sure. I'm not really hungry.'

'Me neither.' He brushed unnecessarily close on his way to the kitchen.

They only toyed with their meal, each pretending to be unaffected by the other, aware darkness had fallen and the apartment grown dim. Elly hardly dared look across the table and barely heard the clinking of cutlery on china and the ticking kitchen clock.

Finally, Rusty spoke. 'You'll miss Molly when she's gone.'

Forced her to look at him, Elly reeled in shock to see the longing in his eyes.

'Yes, I will,' she admitted softly.

'For a woman who claims she doesn't take to kids, you've done rather well.'

Elly gave up eating and pushed her bowl aside. 'Well, Molly's a gem. That helped. And you've done most of the work. But at least now I know how every new mother feels. It takes practice and patience and heaps of time. Which is not hard when they're so cute.' She changed the subject. 'Your job sounds like a great adventure.'

'Outback trips usually are. Have laptop, will travel. I'll be on a property called River Downs,' he explained. When she didn't reply, he added, 'I'll be doing an initial survey and covering a few thousand hectares to get an overview of the property. For the local Aboriginals, the area is the dreamtime birthplace of the mountain range so there are cultural issues to be addressed as well as environmental. I understand there are ancient rock paintings, too. I'm looking forward to seeing them. All up,' he shrugged, 'it should only take a couple of weeks.'

He didn't sound at all distressed to be leaving. In fact, judging by the enthusiasm on his face, he looked eager to be gone. Elly pushed back her chair and rose to her feet. 'Would you like dessert?' She cringed, instantly regretting the words.

His mouth pulled into that familiar larrikin grin. 'You know I do.' His tone turned personal and his innuendo was clear.

'Then perhaps you'd like to get it yourself,' she retorted and gathered up their dishes to stride for the kitchen.

But Rusty ambled toward her from the dining-room into the kitchen, snapping off all the lights as he moved through with all the grace and focus of a wild predator. His actions plunged them into near darkness except for traces of filtered light from the living area windows beyond.

Elly gasped, backed up against the kitchen counter, trapped, Rusty closed the gap between them in two long strides. An arm snaked out and wrapped itself about her waist, so strong he hauled her close before she could protest or muster the will to resist. Elly couldn't escape. Idiot, she told herself, forgetting to breathe. You'd never want to.

The finger of his free hand gathered beneath her chin. 'Relax,' he murmured. Even this close in the dark, his profile was all mysterious rangy shadows. He smelt fresh and faintly spicy. 'I've never fallen for my boss before,' he whispered, his mouth hovering over hers. 'But then you're an exceptional case, Ms George, aren't you?'

'Am I?' Breathing was history. An impossibility. 'Rusty, I don't — '

'You don't what?' His eyebrows arched in question and he nuzzled her nose, Eskimo-style. His warm breath drifted across her hot cheeks.

'We can't,' she groaned.

'Can't?'

'Shouldn't.'

'Why not?'

She scrambled for an excuse. 'Because it will ruin a perfectly good friendship.'

'Admit you feel the spark,' he prompted, daring her to deny it.

Elly knew just by looking at him that she did and was falling in love. Love! How had that happened?

Because he was the perfect height and because their mouths were only a breath apart and because she couldn't wait any longer, Elly took the situation in hand and made it happen.

When they kissed, she felt like she'd come home and found heaven. The world receded and the joy of being wrapped in his arms blanked her mind. Finally, they drew apart.

'That was really something,' Rusty muttered.

'Worked for me,' Elly whispered.

'And it wasn't the nanny kissing the boss.' He leaned closer and kissed her lightly again. 'That was Rusty kissing Elly.'

She understood and nodded but, although the admission of their attraction was a heady discovery, no way could their relationship progress.

Elly was first to leave the kitchen and drift toward her room, falling back across her bed, staring up at the shadows playing on the ceiling. This couldn't be happening. It was madness to get involved.

Next morning, Elly wandered out to find Rusty, as always, feeding Molly. He caught her staring and an awkward moment passed in which each read the other's thoughts.

'Morning.'

'Hi.'

Molly beamed with innocent delight, stretching out an arm to Elly as she sauntered closer. The gesture touched her with a deep surge of tenderness.

'Morning, precious.' She touched a soft kiss to the curls on the top of her head. Planting one anywhere near her sweet messy face would have been hazardous. Elly rescued the wet washer Rusty always kept handy and wiped the child's face.

'Mother hen,' he teased.

Elly longed to brush back the hair off his face or run a hand over his stubbled chin and kiss that strong full mouth. She heaved a wistful sigh. Breakfast and work called.

Work. She cringed at the unappealing thought, splashing milk on to a dish of wheat flakes and backing against the kitchen counter to eat them. Most of it still lay in her briefcase, untouched.

A short time later, she smiled casually at them, blew Molly a kiss and headed for the door. 'Bye, people.'

But Rusty stealthily followed. Because she had a briefcase in one hand, car keys and mobile phone in the other, Elly was cornered and panicked. His farewell kiss was barely a kiss at all, merely the softest brushing of lips, but powerful in effect.

'Hurry home.' He kissed her nose and stepped aside with a devilish grin.

Against her awakened feelings, Elly protested. 'That's inappropriate behaviour.'

Beneath her glare, Rusty raised his

arms in the air as though being arrested. His attitude cooled and Elly felt wretched for her rejection.

'I understand.' He pulled a tight smile. 'My attentions aren't welcome.'

They weren't, but not for the reasons he thought. Ignoring the hurt on his face, Elly left the apartment, hating herself for what she had done. By the time she unpacked her briefcase in her office, her agony had barely dulled. Dallas hovered in front of her desk as usual, ready to deal with her boss's completed weekend's work. Elly produced a few pathetic sheets of paper and handed them over.

Dallas's black eyebrows arched in amazement. 'Is that all you managed?' She nodded. 'Busy weekend?'

'Molly.' Elly cringed at using an innocent child as an excuse.

'Children do have a way of taking up your time.' Her assistant grinned wryly. 'Don't look so guilty. You're the boss. So, you gave Webster the whole weekend off then?'

'Ah, no.' She grew uncomfortable, remembering Rusty's kiss and shuffled the papers still littering her desk.

'This what you're looking for?' Dallas sounded amused, producing her business diary from beneath a stack of files.

Elly smiled weakly and murmured vague thanks.

'So, you two spent half the weekend together?' Dallas persisted.

Elly scowled. 'He does live in, remember?'

'How old did you say this man was?'

Elly squirmed. 'Ah, I guess about thirtyish,' she gabbled really fast.

Dallas's eyes lit up. 'Bit old to be a nanny, isn't it?'

Elly grew defensive. 'Who said there's an age limit? Besides,' she tempered her unease, 'He's excellent with Molly. He'd make a wonderful father.'

Elly winced, realising she had just dug herself a deeper hole.

Dallas chuckled. 'That so? If he's such a catch, I'm surprised he's not married already.'

'He was. Once. He's . . . divorced.'

'Well, marriage isn't easy or half of them wouldn't end up that way. So, he's up for grabs again?' Dallas flashed a loaded smile.

'Don't look at me like that,' Elly warned. 'He's not for me. He wants a wife who stays at home and a dozen kids.'

'You know an awful lot about him after only a week.'

'Only in passing conversation.' Elly darted her a scowl. 'And you'd best consider this one at an end or we'll never get any work done.'

'Yes, Ma'am.'

Mid-morning, Elly became aware of chatter and movement outside her office.

Dallas poked her head around the door. 'You have visitors.'

Elly frowned, not comprehending, then knocked against her swivel chair as she sprang to her feet, self-conscious over her awkward fumbling as Rusty sauntered into her office carrying Molly, filling the room like a burst of warm Australian sunshine.

9

Elly rubbed her thigh where she'd thumped it and limped out from behind her desk, trying to look poised.

'What are you doing here?' She ran a swift eye over Molly, hoping her godchild wasn't ill.

'We missed you.'

Startled by his lowered voice and heartthrob smile, she caught her breath. 'You only saw me two hours ago.'

Elly guessed the potential of a relationship with Rusty but, with so many obstacles to overcome, she squashed her hope and stepped away from him. 'Are you going to visit Rachel now?'

Rusty's flickering gaze told her he noticed her evasion. 'Yes.'

Molly wriggled in his arms. Rusty reached for a blank sheet of paper on Elly's desk, crinkled it up and offered it to Molly, keeping her amused a while longer. 'About this morning,' he began.

She hoped he would tell her it was a mistake and make it easier for them both. 'What about it?'

'You weren't . . . comfortable with the situation.'

'I told you, it was improper and unprofessional.'

He regarded her closely at length. 'Untimely?'

He wasn't making this easy and trying to appear unmoved by him was impossible. Molly dropped the paper and grizzled, saving her from responding.

When Rusty bent for it and straightened, Elly looked him directly in the eye. 'It was nice of you to drop by, but I think little Miss Golding here is keen to see her mother.' She felt proud of smiling despite her heartbreak.

She'd grown accustomed to having Molly in her life and could no longer honestly say that she wouldn't one day want children of her own. But hurting

Rusty would never be on her agenda. She envisioned a future between them and it dampened her pleasure in his visit.

Finally reacting to her signals, Rusty moved for the door. 'When should we expect you tonight?'

Elly rubbed her arms. 'Eightish?'

The elevator doors had barely closed on Rusty and Molly's departure, when Dallas rushed back into Elly's office, her face alive with interest. '*He* is your nanny?'

Bracing herself for teasing and wishing her suppressed feeling for the man could be given freedom, Elly nodded.

'I wouldn't be looking so dismal if I had him to go home to.' Dallas shook her head and her auburn hair gleamed. 'Whatever happened to female nannies, twin sets and flat black shoes?'

Elly managed a grin. 'I believe it's called the twenty-first century, Dallas. And close your mouth, you're drooling.

141

By the way,' she added, 'I'll be late into work Wednesday morning. I'm taking Rachel and Molly home.'

'You'll miss that child,' Dallas quietly observed.

'I surely will.'

For Elly, the remaining days in the apartment with Rusty became an edgy endurance in an effort to resist the man with whom she had fallen in love. His attitude, too, turned remote. She missed his bright cheeky mood and easy friendship, then remembered this was wiser, safer.

On Tuesday night, Rusty packed up the nursery. Next morning, while Elly gave Molly breakfast, he dismantled the portable cot then ferried loads of bags, stroller and belongings down to her car. It was really happening. Rusty and Molly were leaving.

It was hard to recall what her life had been like two weeks ago and she dreaded the thought of returning to an empty apartment tonight. Nervous, Elly just wanted their goodbyes to be

142

done and apprehension settled in her stomach.

'All set,' Rusty announced cheerfully when the time came.

'Do you have everything?' Elly averted her gaze because, this close, he looked irresistible and she nursed green envy that one day some other woman would share his life.

'You can never be sure,' he murmured.

Ignoring his innuendo, Elly strode through the door, Rusty following with Molly. The child was all smiles and energy, grabbing handfuls of his hair as they descended in the elevator. Elly held a tense breath as he strapped his charge firmly into her car seat for the last time.

He gently touched the tip of his finger to Molly's tiny button nose. 'Bye, Angel. You're going to be a heartbreaker one day.'

As if understanding, she smiled and kicked.

Rusty straightened and faced Elly

who had been quietly preparing herself for this moment. She could do it. She could say goodbye without hurting or shedding a tear. She could let this man go.

He caught her hands in his own. 'Thank you for trusting me with Molly.'

'Thanks for helping me out.'

When he leaned closer, her heart raced and her mind numbed. Don't kiss me, she screamed inside. I couldn't bear it. His lips brushed her cheek in an achingly gentle kiss that melted her heart and left her weak.

Rusty heaved his backpack and laptop into the RV, climbing up behind the wheel. He started the engine, gave a casual wave and smile, and drove from the building.

Just like that, he was gone.

She stood for a long quiet moment in the silence. A man like Rusty Webster wouldn't be easy to forget, but she was about to try. A lump rose in Elly's throat. Molly gurgled from her car seat and she remembered she still had her delightful godchild's company a while longer.

'Well, sweetie. We're on our own. Back where we started. What did you think of your nanny, eh? Bit of all right, wasn't he?' Elly climbed in behind the wheel. 'Who would have known when we opened the door on him ten days ago?'

In contrast to her gloomy mood, in hospital Rachel brimmed with happiness, her bag packed by her bed, ready to leave. Apart from favouring her left side and a slight limp, Rachel was steady on her feet and carried her daughter down to the car.

As she edged into a lane of city traffic, Elly said, 'Are you sure you can manage on your own?'

Rachel darted her a long-suffering glance. 'Positive. Home help is all arranged, remember? I'm not immobile. Just tired. I suppose Rusty's gone?'

Elly nodded, pretending to concentrate on traffic.

'Do you expect to hear from him again?'

'I shouldn't think so.' Her admission hurt.

'Would you like him to?'

Elly shrugged and slowed for a red light. 'Our lives run in different directions.'

'But he's got you thinking, right?' She felt her friend's steady stare then Rachel clapped her hands. 'You're in love!'

Elly scoffed. 'After only ten days? Impossible.' She hesitated. 'Besides, he wants a woman who'll happily stay home, barefoot and pregnant.'

'Sounds like heaven to me.'

Elly moaned. 'It's all right for you. You're maternal. And I can't give up my business.'

'Rusty wouldn't expect that.'

'Rachel,' she argued, 'Motherhood is not for me.' The traffic light turned green and they moved off again.

'How do you know until you try?' Rachel challenged.

Fortunately for Elly, the discussion ended when they turned into Rachel's narrow street and pulled into the driveway of her block of flats.

Rachel turned to her daughter in the back seat. 'Molly, sweetie. We're home.'

A spasm of envy clutched at Elly's heart when she caught the child's returning smile in the rear view mirror. Elly helped her upstairs, then ferried Molly and all of their gear from the car.

Elly had expected to feel lost, but nothing like this. Thursday, trying to forget Rusty flying north across Australia, she telephoned Rachel twice from the office only to discover her friend was managing fine. So she plunged herself back into work, grateful that it filled a void where people used to be.

When the telephone shrilled across her apartment that night, she grabbed it, hoping it might be Rachel up for a chat after putting Molly to bed.

'Elly.'

Her heart jumped to hear a familiar

deep male voice and she stifled her delight that he'd called. 'Rusty! I guess you're somewhere in the great Australian outdoors.'

'No. Home actually.'

Elly's pulse performed a small hopeful dance. 'As in Badger Creek?'

'Yes.'

'I thought you had an early morning flight.'

'Me, too. Northern Territory trip's been postponed until Monday.'

Her mind raced. He'd be in Melbourne for three more days.

'How do you feel about a ramble in the country on Saturday?'

It sounded exciting and she ignored all the reasons why she should refuse. 'Where did you have in mind?'

'Is that a yes?'

His voice was impossibly deep and persuasive, and she melted. 'It's a possibility.' But hopelessly unwise.

'We're going bush. Since you're a morning person, I'll come by for you at dawn.'

Dawn! He hung up before she could object.

After Rusty's phone call, Elly realised she'd just made a date and tried to remember the last time she'd had one. Then she realised she shouldn't be seeing him at all. Hard to forget that devilish smile, that tall athletic man moving about the apartment. His shirts scrunched up to the elbow. Sun browned arms and face betraying his outdoor work. Tomorrow would drag in anticipation.

It was still dark when Elly struggled to leave her deeply snug bed early on a frosty Saturday morning. Why on earth did Rusty want to meet at this hour?

When her doorbell rang, she still wasn't ready. Apprehensive, she had skipped breakfast and dithered over clothes. In the end, she wore a peacock blue silk shirt tucked into her favourite faded blue jeans and grabbed a black corduroy jacket in case they were out late and the spring air grew cold.

When the buzzer sounded, she took

deep calming breaths in front of the hall mirror, then lunged forward and opened the door.

The vision of Rusty leaning against the frame, casually wind-messed and gorgeous, took Elly's breath away. Long loose waves of dark hair drifted about his face. A graze of stubble darkened his chin making him look even more rugged and desirable.

His black polo shirt outlined his wide strong shoulders. Light grey cotton pants hugged his hips and were cinched at his slim waist with a black plaited belt.

With a casual smile she said a breathless, 'Hi.'

His slow gaze travelled over her from head to foot. 'Perfect.'

She blushed. The refreshing outdoorsy scent of him filtered into her senses as he caught her hand. With their fingers laced together, they walked to the elevator. Riding down, Elly's heart thumped faster and thought how great he looked and how wonderfully unexpected it was to see him again.

Within an hour, they were heading east on the Maroondah Highway toward the Yarra River valley, approaching green low lying mountains. The further they travelled, the more rows of vineyards emerged, climbing up from the valley on to the edges of hills.

Elly's attention sharpened. 'You live out this way, don't you?'

'What a coincidence.' His smile dazzled.

He was introducing her to his world. 'You still haven't told me where we're going.'

Not taking his eyes off the road, he grinned. 'Wait and see.'

'Are we going to watch some rare bush animal forage for breakfast?' she probed.

He chuckled but, to her annoyance, refused to say.

'We're having a bush barbecue?' When he still refused to be drawn she grumbled, 'Well, I hope this is all going to be worth it. I'm starving.' She, who once avoided it, now looked forward to the first meal of the day.

In the lightening gloom preceding daybreak, they turned off the highway, speeding along secondary roads. The headlights picked out lavender farms, market gardens and vineyards as they cruised past. When they finally slowed and headed through an open gateway and into a small paddock, the sight ahead took Elly's breath away.

She turned to Rusty. 'We're not!'

He grinned. 'We certainly are.'

Vehicles and a ground crew had already begun inflating a striped hot air balloon lying on the ground. The brisk chill of a pre-dawn morning hit them, nipping at their faces and fingers as they climbed from the car. Rusty draped a thick parka about her shoulders. Elly gratefully shrugged into it, zipped it up to the neck and sank her hands into the pockets. She gaped at the whooshing stream of flame from the gas burner and the noisy air fan inflating the balloon.

Rusty stretched an arm around her shoulder and hugged her close. 'Passengers usually check in at the office first while the pilot checks wind speed and direction, but I wanted to bring you straight here to the launch site.'

'Why does it have to be so early?' she asked.

'Because it's calmest while the sun's still low in the sky.'

'Is it safe?'

Rusty squeezed her shoulder. 'Of course. I've been up before.'

Within ten minutes the balloon was fully inflated and one of the crew beckoned Rusty and Elly forward.

She checked her excitement and greeted a man called Ed who Rusty introduced as the pilot. Then they scrambled into the wicker basket and, after a short briefing while he explained procedures, they gently lifted off.

Elly clung to Rusty, her other hand gripping the basket edge tight, awed as the ground fell away beneath them. As they slowly rose higher and drifted with the wind, Elly relaxed, comforted with Rusty beside her and exhilarated at the view.

Now and again, the unobtrusive pilot shot a huge flame up into the envelope, keeping them aloft. Otherwise, it was just Rusty and Elly. No noise. No diversions. An utterly awesome and peaceful experience to share.

Elly hardly dared breathe as they hung seemingly motionless over the green fenced paddocks of landscape spread out below. Time and life slowed with their drifting pace.

As the sun flared above the horizon in an orb of gold, the soft blue morning sky was reflected in water as they passed. The light breeze ushered them over stretches of grape vines, houses hidden in the bush and the basket skimmed the trees on hilltops. They seemed so close, Elly felt she could reach out and touch them. She marvelled at the silence, captivated by the superb unending sight in every direction of hills and shadowed valleys stretching between horizons.

'Enjoying it?' Rusty murmured in her ear.

Elly glanced up at him, nodding, and he kissed her cold nose. This high, the air was freezing. Great for snuggling close which was wonderful, but troubling.

'I don't want it to end either, Elly,' he whispered, reading her thoughts and infusing more into the words than he said.

Too soon, Elly heard the pilot radio his ground crew relaying where they would land. The earth drifted closer to meet them until they landed with a gentle thud. All hands dashed forward to retrieve ropes and anchor them. Their lovely private ride was over.

When the crew had deflated and packed up the balloon, they transported Elly and Rusty back to his RV.

Before climbing in, Elly grasped his arm, smiling. 'Thank you. That was unforgettable.'

'My pleasure.' He flashed a playful

glance. 'Now let's go eat.'

'Food.' Elly groaned with pleasure. 'Lead me to it.'

A short drive brought them to a nearby vineyard restaurant. With golden slits of sunlight winking through fat vine leaves above, they sat outdoors on the terrace, drenched by the strengthening morning sun. They ate piping hot scrambled eggs, crispy fried bacon and sipped chilled champagne.

'What made you decide to organise a balloon ride this morning?' Elly voiced the puzzling question on her mind as she cupped her hands around a welcome first cup of freshly brewed coffee for the day.

'To spend some time with you.' He paused, a worried expression on his face. 'And to give you time and space.'

'Why?'

'Because you need it.' Brown eyes met blue and filled with concern. 'To think about us.'

At this early stage, their relationship was fragile and undefined, but Elly was alerted by the depth of meaning in Rusty's voice.

Warily, Elly carefully chose her words. 'Rusty, after only two weeks, I admit that I'm attracted to you.' She lowered her gaze with the admission.

After an awkward silence fell between them, he prompted, 'But?' And his eyebrows arched in question.

'I have so many doubts and questions. We're so different.'

'They do say opposites attract.'

Elly frowned. 'But what about further down the track?'

'Let's not look too far ahead.'

She looked away across the hills and vines, unable to face the tenderness in his eyes. 'I think we should. It might avoid unhappiness later on.'

When she turned back, it was to witness a heartening smile slowly cross his face, and suddenly the morning didn't seem quite so bleak. 'Don't look so scared. Give it time.'

'How long have I got?' she quipped.

'As long as you want,' he murmured,

reaching across the table and placing his big warm hand over hers.

'But what if I can't give you the answer you want?' she posed softly.

'We'll discuss it when the time comes.' With a rueful shake of his head he chuckled. 'Come on.' He caught her hands and drew her up to stand before him. 'Let's not dwell on it and spoil a promising day. I'll take you to my home at Badger Creek. It's not far away.'

Back on the road in his RV, Elly glimpsed homes nestled among the bush land as they drove, and wondered which one belonged to him.

They turned down into a long gravelled driveway leading to a large and secluded single storey mud brick house virtually hidden from the road by trees, ferns and a natural bush land garden.

He sat for a moment after turning off the engine. 'Welcome to my home.'

Home. Rusty uttered the word with such deep meaning and warmth, Elly realised just how much it meant to him.

He would never give it up to live elsewhere and she would never ask it of him.

'When my work takes me away from this for weeks at a time, I appreciate it even more when I get back.'

He stepped from the vehicle and came around to her side, opening the door. She enjoyed the warm feel of his fingers curled around hers and a refreshing coolness tinged the air.

Birds calls echoed sharply around them. Captivated by her surroundings, for the first time in years Elly actually stood still and absorbed the tranquillity. Amazed at the lack of noise, or hum of traffic, or rattle of trams.

Rusty leaned closer. 'Hope it's not too quiet for you out here?' he teased.

'No,' Elly breathed, afraid to raise her voice and disturb the silence. 'It's so peaceful, with such a lovely natural beauty you'd never find in any formal garden.'

'It's my own few acres of privacy on earth, and today,' he sought her hand

and squeezed it, 'I'm sharing it with you.'

His encouraging revelation filled her with warmth. Elly's impression as they wandered toward the front door was of lush damp ferns, brick paving under-foot, thick solid stone house walls, turned timber posts and the reflected glinting colours of stained glass.

When they stepped inside, she gaped. Massive timber beams stretched overhead, barely outclassed by a huge central open fireplace. Slate floors shone beneath rich floor rugs and deeply comfortable leather sofas. Aboriginal artefacts, bush paintings and other mementos covered the walls.

Elly dropped her denim jacket over the back of a recliner, sank her hands into her jeans pockets and sauntered. This was a home.

'Would you like something to drink?' Rusty rubbed his hands together and started moving through the house.

She half turned back to him from studying an Australian impressionist landscape. 'A strong coffee would be nice. Is this an Arthur Streeton?' She squinted at the signature on the painting, a fan of the Australian impressionist artist herself.

'Snapped it up years ago,' he called out from the kitchen where she soon heard a kettle whistling.

'How long have you lived out here?' She crossed the room and leaned against the open doorway, watching him prepare their drinks, charmed by his familiarity with kitchens including her own.

'Built most of it myself and moved in four years ago.'

His wife would have lived here then, Elly realised. At first glance today, she was captivated by its comfort, originality and understated style.

Rusty stirred milk and sugar into his mug, leaving hers black and rich as she liked it. As he handed it to her, they shared a knowing smile.

His fingers brushed aside a wisp of hair from her face and tucked it behind her ear. 'There isn't anything about you, Elly George, I'm likely to forget.'

She drew in an uneven breath, needing to escape. Hearing a bark, she headed for the wide glass doors letting in light and a breathtaking view across the back of the house. As they stepped out on to the broad covered timber deck, a golden sable Sheltie trotted toward them.

'You have a dog,' she exclaimed with delight.

'Her name is Shae.'

'Hey, beautiful.' Elly leant down and patted her.

The animal hung about their legs while they leaned on the railing and sipped their hot drinks. Below, the land fell away into a gully.

'This is breathtaking,' Elly marvelled as Shae sat down on her haunches between them. Absently, she scratched the dog behind the ears. 'I can see why you love it out here.'

When Shae responded to Elly's attentions with a wet-nosed nudge and a wagging tail, Rusty smiled. 'Looks like you've found a friend.'

For no particular reason, she said softly, 'It's comforting to know you're loved.'

'Yeah. It can be worthwhile.' He turned and fixed his eyes on her for a moment before draining the last of his coffee. 'How about a tour of the house?'

Rusty's pride was obvious and justified. As she peered around corners and wandered along wide naturally lit hallways, her loafers squeaked on the earthy-toned tiles beneath her feet. Because none of the living area windows had drapes, it drew the outdoors in, making you feel secluded and a part of the surrounding bush.

'What do you have planned for the day?' Elly asked with interest.

'I thought we'd stay in and you could cook lunch.'

'Me?' Elly squeaked. 'I can't even boil water. I guess I could toss a salad.' She threw her hands in the air and laughed.

'You'll do fine. I'll be standing right next to you.'

Elly caught her breath and surveyed the compact kitchen. In that confined space? Help. She ignored her qualms. 'I hope you're prepared to be patient.'

Rusty slid an arm around her waist and guided her toward the kitchen. 'Let's go make some food.'

As they chatted, chopped food and drank wine, Elly discovered the new experience of cooking was fun when shared, and it helped that Rusty knew what he was doing. Under his guidance, she cooked the starter while he set the dining table and lit three chunky candles.

After entrée, he leaned closer and kissed her. 'That was delicious.'

'The kiss or the meal?'

'Both.'

A voice in Elly's head warned her not to let her heart rule. 'What's next?'

'I believe we have fillet steaks to grill.'

By the time they'd eaten them and relaxed with more glasses of local red wine, it was time for dessert. Fresh berries drenched in champagne and shared in a glass bowl with two forks.

Relaxed in Rusty's addictive company, Elly staring idly at him. When he caught her gaping, she leapt to her feet and gathered up their dishes. From the kitchen, now suddenly her haven, she saw Rusty snuff the candles and flick a match to the logs in the fireplace. The muted strains of country music drifted in from the stereo.

Rusty reappeared at her side, turned her in his arms and said, 'Dance with me, Elly.'

Helpless to protest, she found herself being led back into the large room. Warm flames, dim light, mood music. She knew a set-up when she saw it. She should resist, but didn't want to be anywhere else.

They melted into each other's arms and with their cheeks brushing, Elly closed her eyes and dreamed. This man, this house, was too perfect and cosy. She contemplated the hectic city life she had always known, then considered the haven and solitude out here. The stillness and quiet, the rustle of dry eucalyptus as a cheeky breeze rushed up the hillside teasing the leaves, the red flash and screen of rainbow lorikeets as they flitted between trees. Privacy. Time.

At that moment, mid-thought, Rusty moved his face a fraction, their noses grazed and their lips met. The music continued but they stopped dancing and kissed instead. Right then, their differences didn't matter and common sense vanished. Rusty Webster was irresistible and she was in his arms where she belonged.

As they broke apart, Elly hauled reason into her mind. Their mutual attraction was exciting, but reality loomed. For Rusty's sake, she must make the sensible choice now before it grew tougher.

She loved Rusty's home and loved that he'd shared it with her, but when he returned from the Northern Territory in two weeks, she must ease him from her life. He wanted and deserved a homemaker. Which she wasn't. So she must release him for the benefit of another more suitable woman. The thought sliced a jealous agonising ache across her heart.

10

By the time the elevator doors slid open and Elly strode towards her office on Monday morning, she had devised a plan for a new project to keep herself busy and stop pining for Rusty Webster.

When Dallas arrived, Elly called her in. 'We're setting up a crèche.' If her own recent experience with Molly was any indication, it was desperately needed.

'No problem.' Her assistant beamed and, without another word, marched from the office and returned with an already crammed file of notes, correspondence and plans. 'I've already checked out the Children's Services Act and Regulations, and applied for a licence.'

Elly sank into her chair and gaped. 'When did all this happen?'

Dallas grinned. 'While you were

making up your mind.'

'What's this?' Elly frowned, pulling a sheet of paper listing many familiar names.

'Our first customers. Mothers have already booked in. I pinned a notice on the board in the tea room to gauge support and you've never seen so many women sign up their preschoolers so fast.' Dallas chuckled. 'Everything's set. We just need to carry out the renovation work.'

'And where exactly is that going to take place?'

Dallas headed for the door. 'Come on, I'll show you.'

Smiling and impressed, Elly pushed back her swivel chair and followed but with her assistant having blitzed the groundwork, her only concern was not having enough left to do to keep her mind off a certain person she needed to forget.

Down the hall, Dallas opened the door into a large but rarely-used utility room. 'We can convert this for the crèche and adapt the adjoining existing kitchenette and bathroom facilities.' She spread her arms wide. 'Picture this. Freshly-painted walls. Bright kiddies furniture. And Monique Dupres, our French language tutor, is a children's book illustrator and she's designed a fabulous mural to cover that entire back wall.'

Rusty would love seeing this, Elly sighed, just before her mobile phone rang, interrupting their dream run. She answered the call, spoke briefly and hung up. 'The language tutors are ready for my meeting. Are we done?'

Dallas nodded. As they left, she paused in the lobby area between the main room and central corridor outside. 'This space is adequate for a small office.'

'I'm going to call you Dallas the Dynamo from now on,' Elly laughed, feeling redundant but also proud of her assistant's initiative and competence. In that moment, the seeds of a possible new direction in the Academy's future were sown in her mind. 'Let's get this crèche underway. I'll read and sign all the paperwork so we can start.'

In the following days, forgetting Rusty proved hard and Elly missed him with a deep confronting loneliness. She dared not think that he might never contact her again and yet was afraid he might.

In her office, she doodled, played solitaire on her laptop and actually left the building for lunch, not returning for at least an hour. At night, she jumped any time the telephone rang out across her apartment and, although her heart leapt in hope, it was never Rusty.

Two weeks later, Elly organised preparations for an official crèche opening.

When the important day arrived, the special decorated cake Elly secretly ordered awed the crowd as it was wheeled in, spiked with lit celebratory sparklers. Toddlers' eyes doubled in surprise, and gasps and applause spread through the gathering.

Elly cleared her throat for a speech. As she proudly looked out over the newly-transformed and colourfully stimulating facility, her heart skipped when she noticed a latecomer sneaking in the door at the back of the room. Rusty.

What on earth was he doing here? And how did he know about today? At the sight of him again looking suntanned and gorgeous, unshaven, wearing outdoor khakis, sunglasses pushed back on his head, every word of Elly's carefully written speech flew out of her head. Forced to ad lib, she conducted the ceremony with physical poise but her mind was a fog.

Then they were cutting the celebration cake and the children clamoured forward for a slice. Noise and chaos overtook the lull.

When Elly's gaze connected with Rusty, he flashed his familiar cheeky smile and pushed through the crowd. Rattled by his reappearance, she stood fixed to the carpet. In the middle of the crowded room, he reached out, drew her close and kissed her. The effects whipped through her like a cyclone.

'That should be good for plenty of office gossip,' he quipped.

'When did you — ?'

'About an hour ago. I called from the airport and spoke to Dallas. She told me about the crèche opening so I jumped in a cab and came straight here. I knew today would be important for you and I wanted to be here.'

Was this man perfect or what? She groaned. Seeing him again eroded all the resistance she'd tried building while he was away.

Rusty's eyes danced over her and his mouth kicked into a smile. 'Can you get away?' he murmured, reaching for her hand.

He wouldn't look so pleased when he heard what she had to say and it couldn't be here. 'My place?'

'Sure,' he nodded, placing a guiding hand at her elbow and steering her from the room.

She tried to feel casual strolling

beside him for the length of the central corridor to the elevator.

Halfway there, Dallas called out behind them, 'Elly, telephone call from Canberra.'

Blast. Her composure wavered. The looming conversation with Rusty was important and couldn't be delayed. Around Rusty, she wasn't sure she'd have the courage to face it again. Looking back to her assistant, she ordered, 'You handle it, Dallas.'

In the elevator, Elly stood apart from Rusty so they didn't touch. In his RV, she swallowed past her dry throat and, to keep the atmosphere neutral, asked, 'How was the outback?'

'Hot and lonely.' He glanced across at her. 'We camped out most of the time. Lived and slept under the stars. We took off in choppers a few times.'

'Sounds fascinating.'

When he spoke of blue skies, red dirt and white-trunked gum trees like it was his second home, all Elly heard was his deep rich voice and how she'd missed it. When he described ochre-faced gorges and clear rock pools, hinting that he'd love to show it to her some time, she filled with a dull ache, knowing it would never happen.

At her apartment, Elly unlocked the door and tossed the keys onto the hall table, Rusty tight on her heels. She didn't offer any hospitality, just moved as far away from him as possible.

She turned to speak and saw the sombre look on his face. She gazed across the chasm between them and opened her mouth to speak but Rusty started first.

Feet apart, hands sunk deep into his trouser pockets, he said softly, 'I've loved you from the first moment you opened your door holding Molly in your arms.'

Oh no, Elly silently pleaded. Don't do this to me. He had just turned a heartbreaking moment bittersweet and shattered her poise.

'I want you with me every day of my life. Marry me, Elly.' He pleaded in a husky voice.

She backed away, gaping at him like an enemy. He'd just bared his soul and it tore her apart but she refused to hurt him like his ex-wife.

'Oh, Rusty,' she whispered. 'You want it all. Marriage. Kids. I can't do it.'

His dark eyes clouded. 'You said you believed in marriage.'

'For other people. Not me.'

'Maybe you just haven't met the right person,' he challenged.

Her longing for him was so strong she almost crossed the carpet and flung herself into his arms. In a few short weeks, he had become her support, her love and her dearest friend.

'You don't love me,' he said heavily.

'No! Oh, no. I love you with all my heart. But I can't deceive and hurt you. I run a company. It's a full time job and I love the work. I don't have time for anything else.' She cringed at how selfish it sounded. She stopped breathing at the longing in his dark eyes. 'You want dozens of kids running around — '

'One day.'

'I can't give you a promise.' Elly's stomach churned to see the ruin on Rusty's face. But he had to know the truth. Now. Not in the future when he'd hate her for concealing it.

'I think you're underestimating your potential. I've seen you with Molly.' He grew still and she sensed he had more to say. 'What if you could have your job and me, too?'

Elly stared. 'How?' She'd already considered a dozen possibilities.

'Commute.'

She shook her head. 'Two to three hours in the car seems an awful waste of precious time every day.'

His big shoulders lifted into a questioning shrug. 'How about you stay in your apartment and come out to Badger Creek at weekends?'

It didn't sound any more appealing than his first suggestion. 'Can't you see, Rusty,' she pleaded, her hands restless, 'I'm not right for you?'

'So, you've made up your mind

already. You won't reconsider?'

She hated to see the desolation in his eyes. Swallowing hard, Elly nodded, too choked to speak.

'You're refusing my proposal? Just like that.'

It sounded simply awful when he put it like that but she slowly nodded, believing she had no other choice.

Looking shocked and confused, Rusty backed away. Amid the crushing ache in her heart, Elly realised she'd actually done it. Turned him away, but she couldn't give him an iron-clad guarantee. No way would she make a hasty promise now and be forced to break it.

'I can't convince you?' he pleaded, his voice low. The anguish on his face almost made her change her mind. She shook her head again.

His shoulders hunched and he turned to leave. 'If you ever change your mind, call me.'

He was leaving! She controlled her panic. Elly watched the tall broad shouldered man turn and heard the soft click of the front door behind him. She waited a few minutes, but the apartment stayed silent and a cold chill of realisation drifted down her spine.

Too desolate to cry, she prowled the apartment, looking around her. Hardly a place to live and raise a family. Whereas out at Badger Creek? She looked down from her windows across Melbourne. Breathtaking. But the views from the windows in Rusty's house were intimate and welcoming.

She tried to contemplate life without him. Impossible. If she continued on alone, nothing changed but love and Rusty would be missing. Could she live with that? No. She wanted him to be the father of her children.

Elly threw her arms up in the air. Finally, she saw her future clearly. She loved her business and loved her work, but she wanted to become a wife and mother, too. Mrs Rusty Webster of Badger Creek.

With her heart pounding and her hands shaking, Elly called Rusty's mobile. It rang out for ages. Finally, he answered.

'I've changed my mind,' she blurted out, her heart pounding.

There was a long loaded silence. 'Be right there.'

Within seconds, the doorbell rang.

Who could that be at this hour when she was trying to sort out the rest of her life? The last thing she needed was visitors. A sense of déjà vu scrolled through her mind. The buzzer didn't stop.

'All right, all right,' she muttered. 'I'm coming.'

Through the peephole, she saw Rusty leaning against the doorbell, smiling. She wrenched open the door. 'How did you get here so fast?'

'I was here all the time.'

'Here?' Knowledge dawned. 'You didn't leave?'

He checked his watch. 'Do you realise, you took five whole minutes? Do you have any idea how slowly time passes when you're waiting for the most important decision of your life?' He gave her a slow smile.

Elly felt like dissolving into tears, but reached out and wound her arms around his neck. 'Oh, Rusty Webster, I need you in my life,' she whispered. 'I love you with all my heart and everything else it's possible to love you with.'

'Me, too.' He brushed her lips in a gentle kiss then cupped his hands around her face. 'Are you quite sure about this?'

'Yes. Eventually, we will have children. I promise.' And she meant it. 'I'll be the best mother a CEO is able to be.'

Then his arms were around her and he kissed her and that was all she needed.

DUET IN LOW KEY

Doris Rae

In their quiet Highland village, the minister, David Sinclair, and his wife Morag, await the return of their daughter Bridget from convalescence. But a newcomer to the village causes Morag some consternation. Ledoux, big and flamboyant, is a Canadian forester, and has caused a stir locally. Morag fears that Ledoux, at a loose end in the quiet community, might make a play for their gentle and innocent daughter — and the potential for scandal would never do . . .

ONLY A DAY AWAY

Chrissie Loveday

When Sally is offered a position in New Zealand, she sees it as the opportunity of a lifetime. Unfortunately, her mother doesn't share her view — and neither does her fiancé. Sadly, she hands back his ring and looks to an uncertain future. When Adam arrives in her life though, along with a gorgeous little boy, everything becomes even more complicated. But New Zealand works its own brand of magic, and for Sally an unexpected, whole new life is beginning . . .

WHENEVER YOU ARE NEAR

Jeanrose Buczynski

After her break up from a disastrous engagement, Sienna Churchill is ready to make the most of life again and flies to Spain to work as a travel rep with a friend. However, six months later she returns home to her father's farm — and makes a shocking discovery when a ghost from the past reappears . . .

YESTERDAY'S SECRETS

Janet Thomas

Recently divorced archaeologist Jo Kingston comes home to Cornwall with her daughter Sophie to live with her father. When her old 'flame', Nick Angove, is injured on a dig Jo takes over, but faces fierce resentment from him. Then, intriguingly, human bones are found and the police become involved. Nick is injured, apparently when disobeying orders, but actually in saving Sophie's life. And as the truth emerges, they begin to acknowledge that their former love has never really died.